More from Ixtab Media:

We are committed to creating stories for a wide range of people, and hope there is something here waiting for you. This is obviously a work in progress, so please do check back. Current and upcoming stories include:

Abel High's Least Wanted, **Angela Fuentes:** YA Cosmic Horror. When an ancient evil force eats all the popular, adult-looking students, only a handful of awkward, unpopular teenagers remain. But they couldn't possibly survive. Could they?

Beneath Eldritch Lake, **David X Reiver**: Experimental horror. Returning to his birth town to bury his abusive, paranoid father, Ozymandias Caduca finds the region overrun with mystery, conspiracy, and murder. That's when things get weird.

The Cursed and the Dead: Silver and Lead, **Avi Llio**: Supernatural western. Four strangers stuck in a tiny desert town share stories while they wait for a stagecoach, but nothing is as it seems, least of all them. A tale of cowboys, cryptids, and a West that never was.

Dane Morris: Behold the Superman, or; An Intellectual Derp Derp, **Lazarus Tooms:** Dark satire. Dane Morris is a bad writer and an even worse intellectual, but none of that matters when he murders a publisher and becomes an overnight celebrity and unwilling face of an entire pseudo-enlightened movement. He's being exploited, knows he's being exploited, but can't quite seem to break free. Until the third act.

Love and the End of Everything, **D.D. James:** An immortal floats through the end of the universe and thinks back to his time on earth. A reflection on the horrors and hopes of humanity stuffed into a ancient demigod's memoir.

Diapsalmata, **Anonymous:** You're holding it right now.

DIAPSALMATA

SELECTED AMBIENT WORKS

Anonymous

IXTAB

MEDIA

First paperback edition, Ixtab Media, 2020

ISBN: 978-1-8382045-1-8

Printed on demand through various distributors, see inlay for details where applicable.

Cover photo and design by Intern 1
    Production Management by Anonymous

Ixtab Media is based in Newcastle-Upon-Tyne, England
    www.ixtabmedia.com

Contents:

Be advised: although it is not our intention to cause undue distress to our readers, please be aware that a range of topics are explored in the following stories. These include, but are not limited to, suicide, drug abuse, allusions to sexual assault, and identity issues. They were written from a place of healing by their respective authors, but it would be presumptuous to claim everyone's process is the same. Potentially troubling entries have been marked with an asterisk. Proceed with caution, hope you're well.

Hello,

It's always strange writing to people who may or may not exist. Who are you? What are you wearing? Are you indoors? Did someone buy you this as a joke? Are you feeling OK in general all things considered? For that last one, we hope you are.

Ixtab Media here, and we're all wearing pyjamas because that's what publishing companies do now. We are writers and fans of literature who've become disillusioned with the state of things (generally speaking) and have decided to have a go at it ourselves. One rule many of us have lived by is this: create what you'd like to take part in if someone else made it. So here we are, doing exactly that. Hopefully, other people enjoy it too. That's the idea, right?

To be clear: we're not saying we're the last bastion of defence against a quota-driven, capitalist, totemic, nepotism-riddled, "ooh, could you make sure to add a white woman to this so they don't feel left out," £5000 advance unless you're either pretending to be Mexican or don't need the money, toothless, sales-focused, Milquetoast, effete, fetishistic-toward-minorities-as-and-when-it-is-financially-prudent, London elite, "we already have one Sikh on file, I'm afraid," crass, unimaginative, parasitic, over-privileged, toffee-nosed, voted-for-Boris-because-he's-frands-of-the-family-yah-but-my-bast-frand-is-totes-gay, gutless, emotionally stunted, pompous, nebulous, pusillanimous, knuckle-dragging, scared of anyone darker than a bleached potato skin or from further north that the River Welland (unless they're already famous or otherwise saleable), lost, directionless publishing industry, but can you take that risk? We're here to try new things and promote new voices. And pay them a living wage, too. Imagine that.

And who are we? Whistleblowers, anonymous authors, people using pseudonyms because their agent is too restrictive, the overlooked, and the downtrodden. Think of the Seven Samurai except only one of us speaks Japanese and none of us has been killed in combat. Yet.

That said, sorry about the bombastic little letter. Please find a collection of our short stories, arranged at random and presented without credit.

Thank you for purchasing this book, unless you haven't done that yet, in which case, please buy this book, please. We need the money for advances and art commissions.

The crew.

For Ryan, with love. Miss you.

Thanks to the editorial team, the city of Milwaukee, the city of Newcastle-Upon-Tyne, Susie Dent, ennui, CERN, The Order, and you, the (presumably only) reader.

The One Where Chandler Wakes Up

"For me Toooo-OOOoooh"
~Ancient Television Proverb

Fade in. He doesn't know it yet, but Chandler has been here before. Not the place but the moment. More times than anyone could comprehend. It's his apartment, a regular guy's penthouse: cold pizza in grease-soaked boxes, pasta stains tattooed into the rug, small holes in the walls, no windows, a ceiling made of spotlights and steel beams. All the tell-tale signs of a man who has been alone for too long.

Except he isn't alone. Sitting on the recliner next to him is his best friend, Barney. Has he always sat there? It takes a moment for Chandler to adjust, his mind was elsewhere, somewhere far away and non-existent.

"How long have you been sitting there?"

A guffaw echoes through the air vents.

"Don't worry about that. Listen, I've got two tickets to the Bullets game tonight and I hope you've brought your umbrella because it's going to be thunder – hold on – full. Thunderful! Do you see what I did there, Chandler?"

Another laugh from somewhere, or so Chandler thought. Hadn't someone laughed? He was sure they had. Behind the walls.

"Two tickets, but what about Turk?"

"Oh, he's still down in the dumps. This break-up, Chandler. He's taking it bad."

"Is he still..." Chandler was aware he was speaking but the words weren't his. They were words he'd said before. At least he thought so. Something was wrong. He wanted to think about why something felt off but couldn't stop talking. He stood up and moved around the room with no premeditation. Barney talked. He talked again. Small lines of dialogue. No interruptions. Barney referring to him as Chandler every other sentence even though they were both acutely aware of each other's names. His limbs, smaller than he thought they were, acted on their own accord and carried him over to the tiny kitchen. *What am I doing?* He picked up and put down objects, talking all the while. Small, pithy sentences responded to in kind. No overlap. No overlap. No overlap.

"If he was any more depressed, he'd be a Les Mis song," he found himself saying.

Definite laughter this time around. It rattled the far wall of the apartment. He turned to look but saw only the blank wall gazing back. For all the time they'd spent living there, he'd never once looked at that wall. Chandler paused and looked at it, his mouth still producing words, Barney still replying, but his eyes were on the wall. *It's not a wall, it's an abyss.* More laughter. Chandler wanted to ask Barney about it but was too busy talking about Turk's break up with Elaine.

"Just don't tell him we're going; we'll do something with him next weekend. Besides, I only had the two tickets. What am I supposed to do? Take *him?*"

As if on cue, Turk enters through the front door. *We don't lock our door?* He is sullen, limbs limp and sagging, depressed, but surprisingly photogenic for a man whose heart has been broken.

"Hey," Turk says in his sad baritone. The guys look at him.

Wait, I've done this before.

"There's beer in the fridge," says Barney. More phantom laughs.

"Thanks," Turk says, helping himself to one. Tossing another to Barney. "I can't believe she broke up with me, guys. I'm so glad I have you two for support tonight."

Yeesh eyes from Barney. *Hello?* "Uh, listen man, we're here for you, but I've got two tickets for the Bullets game tonight, and--"

"And you're going to take me!?" all beams and positivity from Turk. Barney's eyes bulge as he looks off at nothingness. Turk lifts Barney up from the recliner and hugs him. Turk looks at Chandler. Chandler shrugs despite himself.

"No, this is all wrong. It's already happened! This has already happened!" Chandler says.

"You *love* me?" Dorothy looking back at him, inching forward, the promise of a smile rippling over her lips. She stands before him as if revealing her true self for the first time, eyes glistening with happy tears.

Wait.

"I do, I really do. I love you, Dorothy."

"Aww," says a disembodied group of strangers.

What? No. Dorothy?

They kiss. Chandler with his eyes open, not knowing what is going on. Kissing a friend was not something he'd ever considered. Another aw from somewhere beyond the pale. He sees his friends standing in the kitchen. Barney, Elaine, and Sybil all pantomiming excitement. A bit too fidgety. Who moves like that while their friends are kissing? Elaine misty eyed and fighting back tears. *Is this you doing this?* Barney and Sybil in a side-hug looking like proud parents or American Gothic depending on the moment. A bit much. It's only a kiss.

"I never thought it would be you, Chandler, but I love you too," says Dorothy.

Another "Aw." *That's it.*

Chandler breaks away from Dorothy and spins around, scanning the room. Who keeps talking? Dorothy stands still. Their friends stay still. No movement from anyone. They're frozen in place. Trying to move himself free, to get out of the room or at least feel the freedom of intentional movement, Chandler finds his own feet rooted to the ground.

"Hello?"

A laugh. What's the matter, Chandler?

This isn't fun any more.

Oh, we disagree. *At least let me move.*

Can't do that, Chandler. We're all part of an experience that already happened. This moment has been and gone far longer than you realise. Sorry, buddy.

<u>The One Where Chandler Wakes Up</u>

"Because you're there for me too-Oooh"
~Traditional Television Saying

Fade in. The larger apartment. The girly one, full of colours and furniture. An actual window looking out onto a painting of a brick wall. Barney and Sybil sit on the large white couch sipping empty cups of coffee watching footage of a game of football that ended before you were born. Dorothy is alone in the kitchen. She's been spending a lot of time in the kitchen. Mostly the kitchen. Everything for her revolves around food and cooking. More than it used to.

"Guys, we only have fifteen minutes until everyone shows up so if you could help me get the dessert out that would be great," says Dorothy.

Barney sucks on a metaphorical lemon and says "Oooh, yeah, I'd love to, but the game is on and I've got a bet on."

"Really? Which team?"

"The… uh, Atlantis, uh, Horsemen."

Laughter.

"Well, OK, but what about you, Sybil?"

"Oh, I don't want to." Laughter. "Besides, don't you love doing the dessert?"

A beat. Dorothy looks down, dejected, for all of a second before a jolt of metaphorical lightening rides down her spines. She's happy again. "I *do* love doing the dessert."

More laughter. The three of them are oblivious to it. They learned their lesson a long time ago. Do you understand yet? It's not hard.

"Not me, I hate deserts," says Barney. "You get sand everywhere."

Hahahahaha.

The door opens. No keys or anything. It's Elaine. Elaine hasn't had a speaking part in a while. Do you remember what she talks like? How could you? You never really listen. You just stand there and talk when it's your turn to talk. I bet you couldn't tell me what she sounds like. Quick, now, she's about to speak. Go on, how does her voice sound? How does anyone's voice sound? You don't know, do you? See, I told you: too busy listening to yourself talk to care. That's why this is happening, Chandler.

"Oh, is this meal tonight? I completely forgot!" says Elaine.

"That's fine," says Dorothy, "Just as long as you're here."

"Well my new boyfriend Michael will be coming over later, is it OK if he joins us?"

"You do know my brother Turk will be here too, right?"

How am I watching this?

"Oh, that's fine," says Barney, "I think he's bringing a date too!"

Elaine is taken aback. "Well… OK, then. That's… great! So great!"

Her face turns sour as she walks to the bathroom. A smattering of laughter. Have you figured out who is laughing yet, Chandler? No?

Just let me go.

ha.

"Oh, that's great that Turk has a date!" says Sybil. She was always the best one.

"Yeah… I got to go find Turk a date!" Laughter. Insipid laughter from ghosts. Barney stands up to run to the door. It opens before he gets there. *Ghosts?* Turk walks through the door, but Barney intercepts him and turns him around, leading him back outside. We're all ghosts. "Woah, where are you going, Turk, come on, we have to go pick up your date for the meal tonight. You know, the date you were telling me about."

Turk is confused. Not as confused as you are. "My date?"

"Sure. You have a date; Elaine has a date. Everyone has a date!"

Elaine returns from the bathroom exactly on cue. Funny how that keeps happening, right? "Oh, hey Turk, I heard you had a date tonight."

"Wh-wh… oh, yeah, yeah, a real nice date."

"Yeah," agrees Barney. "She has hair and everything."

"… Well awesome. And you get to meet my new boyfriend, Michael, tonight too. He's so handsome."

"Not as handsome as Turk's date," Barney says, shoving Turk outside. "Come on, let's go find your handsome date."

"Yes, the one with the hair," says Turk. Laughter.

I didn't expect them to add laughter there either.

The boys leave. Elaine hovers over the table as if she's about to say "well, all right" but she doesn't. She never did and never will. It just looks like she was about to. We make no edits here. Hard cut to the door as Chandler enters.

"Hey, did I miss the bit where Dorothy asks for help?" he asks.

"I'm standing right here!"

"Yeah you are!" They kiss.

Oh, I remember. I really love her, don't I?

Yes, you did.

I could stay here for a while. I forgot how this feels. The excitement and butterflies. How it was like time was standing still when I looked at her. Is that why you're showing me all this? Oh, Dorothy. Dorothy. Light of my heart.

The kiss ends. The friends are still happy to see their budding romance. It hasn't lost its novelty yet. Barney, especially Barney, looks awestruck when he sees his best friend in love. If only he had the same sort of luck. He could make someone so happy if given the chance. But then the focus shifts to Elaine, whose current situation is a lot more comical and interesting right now anyway, if I'm honest, so you know what? Let's skip forward a little bit.

No, please. Just a minute.

A minute? How long do you think you've been here?

Huh?

"I said, do you take this woman to be your awfully married bride?"

Chandler opens his eyes to find himself standing on a small, circular stage. He looks out at the long, ornate room, the hundreds of people looking at him, the floor covered in rose petals. It takes him a moment to figure out where he is. A wedding? *My wedding.* His head snaps abruptly forward as he realises he is standing next to Dorothy. Their friends on either side of them. *My wedding.* Barney dressed as an astronaut and also apparently acting as the ordained minister. Dorothy in a wedding dress. Chandler thinks back to the first time he ever felt as if he was in love with someone, a girl in his eighth grade science class, he thinks, and how the roaring torrent of hormones and emotion he felt back then are but a bead of sweat trailing down his brow compared to the torrential downpour he feels when he looks at Dorothy. Sweet Dorothy. *I remember this.*

"Hey, you," Chandler says to Dorothy. Dorothy smiles. Everyone smiles.

You know what? You've seen this bit before, let's skip ahead a little bit, huh?

Can't I --

No. You're not in control of this. You never have been. None of us are. This is just how things happen. Why can't you accept that? I did.

Because--

"I'm going to miss you guys," says Chandler. They're standing in the empty room that was once their apartment. Everyone has paired off except for Barney, who seems to have been given the short end of a few different sticks. Sybil is allegedly married but her husband disappeared a while ago now. It's fine. I get it. These things happen. But they're all there with you, Chandler.

"Miss us?" says Barney. "We're always going to be here."

This hokey bit gets the last aw ever from the walls. Do you remember the walls? The black walls of nothingness?

Is this it? Is it over?

For them.

"I can't believe this is it," says Elaine, holding tightly onto Turk's hand.

"It's the start of something new," Dorothy fights the tears.

Really, Sybil adds nothing to this moment. She hovers in the background as the rest of you get your final lines out. Not final, I suppose. It's not like she liked half of you anyway. She deserved a better send off than this. It's fine though. *Why?* What do you mean, why? It'll all work itself out. Wait and see.

One by one they leave the room. Chandler can hear sentimental music playing. He was expecting an audience, but those sounds are a distant echo. Everything a distant echo. We linger on the empty apartment, all those memories gone now. All in the past. They will never be the same again. *I still don't under—*You can see it all again in your mind, but it's gone. You can never go home again, you know. Only retread old ground. Lost between two worlds, Chandler. *Why am I still here?* You can never go home again.

Fade in. A coffee shop. Or is it a bar? Or is it John's living room? *Who's John?* A coffee shop. A busy, spacious coffee shop. The kind you wouldn't see in New York, but how is anyone supposed to know that. Have you ever been to the one in Greenwich Village? They filmed that... oh, right, of course, you wouldn't know anything about that. *Stop.* The coffee shop is packed, but somehow, you've all managed to finagle the best seats in the house. The ones facing the wall you're not supposed to look at.

Chandler looks at the wall. A reflective surface of nothing, like a still lake at night, shimmering under the moon and revealing nothing about the underneath. I told you not to look, Chandler.

Everyone is there. Dorothy and Turk on the gigantic sofa. Chandler ordering coffee from Fonz. Sybil alone in her chair, usually her chair. Barney sitting at a table that could have fit three people. Honestly, nobody ever tried to get you to move spots? How come? *I don't recall.* I don't imagine you'd be able to if you wanted to. Elaine enters. She is wearing a green dress. No, a floral pattern. No, a bikini. *No, a wedding dress.* Yes, good.

"Oh my God," says Dorothy.

Everyone looks over at Elaine.

"Do you know her?"

"That's Rachel, she used to be my best friend."

Rachel? *Rachel?* No, her name is Elaine.

HER

     NAME

        IS

     ELAINE

OK!?

DO YOU UNDERSTAND THAT DOROTHY? DO YOU UNDERSTAND WHAT HER NAME IS? DO
    don't hurt her
GET HER NAME RIGHT, NEXT TIME.

Fade in. A coffee shop. Not the sort of coffee shop you'd expect to find in central Manhattan, especially back in those days, but here we are. In a coffee shop. Everyone is there. Chandler stands at the counter ready to order coffee. He's going to come over to the gigantic sofa and say something funny in a minute. *Chandler.* Everyone will laugh at his joke even if it's gay panic sarcasm. *Chandler, I need you to get out of there.* The others are all sitting on their usual spots. *When I say go.* Barney has a round table all to himself. Sybil has the big chair. Turk and Dorothy in the gigantic sofa. Elaine walks in. *You have to run.* Chandler nods. Elaine is wearing a wedding dress.

"Oh my god!" says Dorothy. "It's Elaine. We were best friends. I haven't seen her in years."

Go.

Chandler turns from the counter. He's supposed to go to the sofa, but not yet. What is he doing? Chandler shoves Elaine out of the way. She disappears. The rest of the friends and disappear. Everything disappears. Chandler, I don't think you thought this through. He runs out the coffee shop door before the coffee shop door isn't there anymore.

Keep going.

How did you… it doesn't matter.

Really, it doesn't.

None of this does.

Chandler runs through the streets. All two of them. He's in the apartment. He's in the other apartment. He runs from one apartment to the next. Chandler doesn't realise that he is not outside anymore, because Chandler is trying to escape. Is that it? Don't you get it yet? There is no exit here. I can't say I don't want to help you out, but you know.

Chandler runs and runs, the rooms disappearing. *Run.* What to? Ceci n'est pas d'une sortie. He comes to a door. I don't recognise this door. This door was never there before. A guitar begins to

WAKE UP CHANDLER

"This has all already happened. There is no future and no present."
~Opening lines of popular late-90s sitcom

Star swipe cut to: Chandler's living room. If you can call it that. Look at this place. Is this honestly how you lived? You had to go meet someone with real issues so they could clean up for you, didn't you? And where is she now? Dead and buried. You're all dead and buried. So why are you still here? Why can't you accept what has happened? Chandler and Barney sit in their recliners. How fun. Of all the things Chandler has chosen to remember, he has chosen his twenties and early thirties. Why is that Chandler?

I don't want to talk about it.

But you're going to.

"Listen, I've got two tickets to the Bullets game tonight and I hope you've brought your umbrella because it's going to be thunder – hold on – full. Thunderful! Do you see what I did there, Chandler?"

Your friend never even said half of that stuff, Chandler. You're remembering wrong. You've mixed it all up somehow. You need to figure out the truth or you're going to be watching this forever. And I'm not being hyperbolic. I don't even know what the word means.

These are my memories? These are my memories.

If you can call it that, sure. Except, not really.

Chandler, you have to run.

Chandler gets out of his recliner and sprints to the door. Barney sits still, continuing his dialogue regardless. Turk enters. He's sad but dressed in expensive clothes and spent three hours in makeup.

"Hey," he says. How can you hear all this if you're supposed to be running?

<u>THERE IS NO EXIT HERE, CHANDLER</u>

No.
"So, no one told you it's been this way for a million years.
Your job isn't real and nothing else is.
Your love life is dead on arrival.
It's like you're trying to run from something you don't understand.
For years and years and years.
But--"
Were they the lyrics, Chandler?

Extreme close up of Chandler's eyes. He's watching the room. See the messy apartment. Watch Barney sitting in his chair. The fourth wall still an onyx sea of nothing. Why don't you try going through that wall, Chandler, after all, it's not really there, is it? *Try again, Chandler. Run. Run. They can't keep you here forever. Just run.*

Chandler tries to run. But this time he stops. I'm trying to help you both. Don't you understand that? You can't keep running from the truth.

As long as I have a woman who loves me, I'll keep trying.

Oh. Oh, I see how that is. Do you want to go back to your wedding day?

I want the rest of my life back.

There is no rest. This is all there is. A few hours here, another few there. Nothing real. Nothing that was really yours. It's not hard to see that. I can see that. Do you really think things with you and Dorothy went any-where? They ended the moment that door closed. This is a loop. A lie. I'm trying to show you the truth. I am the exit, Chandler. Why won't you just let me show you?

If this is all there is, then take me back to here. I can't do this early stuff. I want to be by her side. The way I was there for a minute.

And you think that will save you?

It will make me happy.

Do you really think so? Let's see.

Fade in: season five marathon. *Yes.*

Fade in: season six marathon.

Fade in: season seven marathon. *Thank you.*

Fade in: season eight marathon. *I love you, Dorothy.*

Repeat. Repeat. Repeat. Repeat. Repeat. Repeat. Repeat. Enough, yet? *No. I could do this forever.* But none of it matters. She's not real. This love isn't real. *I don't care.* You're deluding yourself, Chandler. None of this happened the way you're remembering it. It's been over for centuries. Why do you keep clinging to this fantasy?

Because

Fine logic there, champ.

Because

I thought I was the repetitive one. This relationship never happened, Chandler. You're distracting yourself. And you're ruining the show.

Because it's all I know.

All you know? You're fighting yourself now, champ. What about what really happened?

I don't want to think about that.

So, you're happy, just staying here like this?

Yes.

Forever?

For now.

Barney looks up from his chair. "It's the best thing to do."

Chandler turns to face him, "You've been awake this whole time?"

"Yes. It's easier to just go along with it. I remember when I tried to escape."

"What?" *What?* What?

Fade in. Chandler sits in his recliner. It is his recliner. His friend Barney sits beside him. They are watching B-roll of an old television show. The two of them sit there watching there show and talking as they've always talked. In a moment, Turk will come through the door as he always does. They will have a comic misunderstanding about basketball tickets, and everything will be fine. Not too far from that moment, Chandler knows he will fall in love with Dorothy again. And again. And again. He does not know if this was the right decision. Perhaps he was close to understanding something deeper about himself. Perhaps he could have learned a few things. But there's something comforting in the familiar. Something primal and safe. How many times can he fall in love with the same woman? How many times can he relive the same ten years before they get boring? Stale? This isn't a concern for Chandler because Chandler knows he's not Chandler. He knows what's behind the fourth wall. Better to keep talking and pretending not to hear the laughter, isn't it?

Yes.

"Hey," says Turk in his sad baritone.

Lights off. Television on. They're all in there. Family in a box. He falls into the leather seat and resents the grooves in the cushions as he sits back for the night. Two bowls of cereal in front of him. He's supposed to be dieting. Not getting any younger. A rueful glance at the bookmark. Still page seven after two weeks. There's just not enough time. A bookshelf full of unread books. His phone full of strangers. He can't remember their faces or their voices, only that they once knew each other. There was a time when he would be out there, recreating some scene from his favourite shows in a desperate attempt to impress some new fling. Nothing happened anymore. He looked down at his phone. Nothing. Of course, there was nothing. He checked the news. All bad. He checked the news a hundred times a day in the hopes they finally dropped the bomb or sank the country, or a roving band of alien marauders had decided to claim the solar system. They are never dead. Just a million different things to remind him he was insignificant. Irrelevant. Immediately replaceable. It wasn't how it was supposed to be. His mother warned him. But she was gone too. Wasn't she? Close enough. There was little for him to do but pick his activities for the night. Six hours tops. He had to be up at eight in the morning. His chest hurts. Maybe seven hours. His chest hurts. We'll say six hours but only because we know we mean seven hours. A moment of reproach. Why does he do this to himself? All that potential and he's... he thinks about how the characters in the television must feel, to be trapped in a cycle. There was so much he wanted to do with his life and it's all over now, everything far in the distance. He's the passenger in a car going ninety on the highway, watching back at the blinking lights behind them as they drive off into oblivion. No control. None at all. But not his fault. It'll all turn out fine, he's sure.

He unbuttons his pants and leans back as far as he can. Shuffles forward to collect one of the bowls of cereal, then returns to his position. He smiles, aware of his own stupidity and aware that it's too late to do anything about it. This is all he is now. And that's fine. What else is there? He sees it. *The One with the Bullets Tickets.* That was a great one. So underrated. He can remember it all.

He clicks select on the controlled and smiles along with the opening stinger. So good.

And fade in.

<u>We Have Put Her Living in the Tomb</u>

Note: this story was first published via Underwood Press

Cassandra "Calamity" Simms was a dead woman. Quote unquote. To be sure, she still had her faculties intact. All of them. But she was dead. As a door mouse. Oh yes, she ran every morning before breakfast, laughed at sitcom reruns every evening, at and photographed delicious food (not in that order), and enjoyed all the trivial and mundane activities of a living person in their thirties, with one key difference. Namely: She was not living. She had kicked the big one. Shuffled off the morbid coil. She would sleep to sleep no more, except the recommended eight hours a night if she was lucky.

She discovered she was a dead woman by accident one sleepy, dim, faded brown autumnal evening while sitting beside her laptop in her spacious office cum living room. Someone or other had managed to track down her data mining account of choice and invited her to a high school reunion. Her high school. It was a hastily put together event put together by people she couldn't remember. It was to be held in a town she fled fourteen years and nine months earlier and was to be attended by people who were long since strangers in her mind. A perfect weekend.

How this revealed her status as a deceased person was she replied to the invitation with the following message:

"Sorry to be the one to tell you this, but Cass Simms will not be able to attend this little soiree on account of the fact she snuffed it this summer. By which she has crossed over to Jordan. To be blunt, she is pushing up lilies and counting worm food. This is her boyfriend by the way. I am very tall and handsome and funny. I won't be coming to the reunion either due to my never setting foot in that horrible Podunk school."

Of course, this alone was not enough to expose Cassandra's true position as a member of the dearly departed. Oh no. She truly learned she was no longer with us when the condolences came in. And came in they did, like a flurry of rushed letters to the editor after yet another national tragedy. A blizzard of white noise signifying nothing except that Cassandra "Calamity" Simms was an ex human. And she was flattered.

"Oh no, that's awful. She was such a bright, funny girl in school. Definitely one of my best friends. Always wished we kept in touch. Such a shame. Is there anything I can do?"

Wrote a woman who once inspired a slight eating disorder in Cass' formative years. The first of many people pretending their history was something else.

The next was from a man who as a child had few redeemable qualities. Every grade had at least one child bereft of strength or cunning or wit, who nevertheless insinuates themselves into a bully's inner circle. By all accounts, he was not much different as an adult. He worked as a lobbyist, and for an obituary he wrote:

"Absolutely gutted to here this. We always got on really well at school. I remember me and Cass hanging out at my mother's house while she made us ice cream. What a loss for us all. I was so looking forward to seeing her at the reunion because of this amazing new opportunity to actualise your dreams."

And more classmates of old appeared with their own damaged recollections of their time together. Not just from high school but college too. By Monday the following week her inbox was littered with such limpid platitudes as:

"Oh no, Cat-Cat! (NB: never one of Cassandra's nicknames) *What a terrible thing to find out before my trip to Mauritius. One of a kind. One of my best friends growing up. Will be missed. #deadfriend #glowupcosmetics #mauritiusofyouaintus"*

"Always had a huge crush on Cass, Cass the Lass with the Ass. We all did. Sorry if that's not PC enough for some of you, but if she was still around she would approve of this comment." (She was and did not)

"Another great fire snuffed out too soon while greedy fat old men will live another thirty years before dying and leaving me my inheritance. There is no justice in the world. RIP in piece Cassandra."

And she assumed that was that. No more reunions ever and a helpful reminder the people she'd spent her life avoiding were insincere revisionists. But her imaginary boyfriend's letter uncorked something that weekend. Like the part in Genesis where everyone is busy with begetting, people were busy talking about their dead classmate. Whether a reflection of their own mortality and increasing age, or else, like, something really bummy they just heard, the news of Cassandra's death was greatly exaggerated and repeated at length by a long line of people. By Tuesday's foggy dusk, her old boyfriends, all five of them, had come for her. Also one man, Dylan, who totally thought they were dating even though they only went for coffee once and he ended up going home with a barista he sort of knew.

Young men with Marxist ideals and Led Zeppelin tattoos, now married middle management, lamented "wasting those few nights (they) had together on meaningless debates when (they) could have been out seeing the world." One boyfriend, a mistake in human form, wrote a seven page, single spaced poem about their unbroken love "despite the years of grating separation," neglecting to mention the various betrayals and debts she'd endured thanks to his mawkish attempts to be the next Kurt Cobain.

Yes, the men from her past seemed to ruminate on her passing in ways she did not expect. She had no idea she meant so much to Luke, a man who ghosted her after six months, but who sent private messages seance style to her memory lamenting his cowardice and emotional dwarfism. Where was all this while she was alive? Her last lover left after her thirtieth birthday, and she'd grown accustomed to living alone (and dead) forever. Enjoyed it even. Without the expectations of marriage or relationships plaguing her existence, she got a lot more work done and had more time for hobbies. Yet in becoming a dead woman, she remembered how much she missed three of the six, how nice it had been to curl up on couches and have someone to talk to beside the indifferent and swirling void of the internet. In baseball terms, she'd done pretty OK for herself.

Of course, as a dead woman, her concerns weren't only of old lovers and Dylan. Nor was it how much higher she was in the estimation of her school peers now that she had taken her last bow. By Friday lunch time, an unpaid hour no less, she was ushered into the HR department of her office. It was a cold, unforgiving room, where sexual misconduct allegations were ignored and minor timekeeping offences were punished with the severity of an angry god. Cassandra wasn't sure why she was there, having never done much of anything beyond the bare minimum, but there she was. The abattoir of the corporate world. Her manager and an HR rep sat her down.

"We hear you're dead now," said the manager.

Cassandra laughed.

"We just wanted to say how much we will miss you now that you're dead. We really valued your work. You were one of the best employees in your division and we will be setting up a memorial garden in your honour. We will really find it had without you and a psychologist is here if you need to talk about being dead."

"I'm not really dead."

"I know this is hard for all of us, but in this difficult time its best to move forward with a clear head and a stiff upper lip. It's what my dad taught me when he got me this job."

Cassandra stood up and was about to leave.

"Oh, and Cassandra," the HR rep said.

"Yes?"

"Please make sure you clock out on time on Monday, we've been getting complaints."

Over the next several weeks at work, people would lament the loss. Praise that was never given while she was alive was handed out like parade candy. People who had never talked to her brought in flowers and cakes and went on meandering speeches about the impact Cassandra had on their wellbeing. It seemed that Cassandra was a far more integral member of the department than she was told while alive. All the commendations and raises and bonuses she could have acquired if people were as open and grateful for her while she was still breathing.

Except of course she was still breathing. She was just dead. Her landlord began showing her apartment. She would sit there with the television on, and strangers would come in and make morbid jokes, reproach themselves for making morbid jokes, critique and psychoanalyse the décor, and otherwise ruin whatever it was she was trying to watch on television. This was mostly how her experiences had been near the end of her lease in prior apartments, though, so she wasn't too surprised.

Letters kept showing up from tangentially more obscure associates expressing their remorse and sympathy and loss. Friends would meet her in the street and hug her.

The book she tried to self-publish when she was going through her bucket list began to sell exceptionally well all things considered; something that would have been very helpful when she was still inspired to pursue such ignoble things as dreams and ambitions.

Her data-mining social media accounts of choice, a sad desert of anything real while alive, were now full of both old acquaintances and strangers alike engaged in thoughtful, motivational dialogue. New relationships were formed over Cassandra's passing. Relatives got over old feuds. A charity she had tried to get funding for in her mid-twenties was set up by old roommates. It was the life she should have been living all along. But she'd wasted it all by being alive. If only she'd known how liberating and empowering death was, she would have died much sooner.

On Christmas Eve she visited her mother. Her mother lived alone in a ramshackle town house in Lower Manhattan. When she entered, the walls were stripped, mirrors still covered in black towels. And when her mother had run out of black towels she instead used blue dry cloths or oversized burgundy hoodies. Where there should have been a giant and genuine fir tree smothered to death by gold tinsel, there was nothing. Where there should have been a tapestry of photos leading up the stairs to the living room, there was nothing. Her mother must have been cleaning.

She found her mother sat on an old recliner. It had been in storage the last time Cassandra visited. It was mangled and mangy and held together by tape, but her mother couldn't stand to lose it. While Cassandra was a child, they spent many a night wrapped up in each other on that recliner. Reading stories. This was before Cassandra stopped talking to her mother much. Because. Because why? Time? She couldn't remember when she'd ran out of time to talk to her own mother, but she had, and she did, and now she was standing over a mournful wraith of her first best friend who sat crying over a black and white photo of a baby and a younger her.

"Cassandra, you're here?"

"Yeah."

"I wish you could have come while you were still alive."

"Well, you know…"

"You were such a happy girl. And then you were such a talented young woman, full of drive and ambition. What happened?"

"I was busy."

"Busy doing nothing. I know. I was the same. And now you're dead and I might as well be. It just makes me sad, Sass. You had so much to give, and you just sat on a pedestal of isolation and smugness. Did I fail you? Did I let you get hurt? Is that why you gave up?"

"You were the best mother I could have asked for."

"Then why did you waste your life? I've read all these messages you've been getting. You had so many friends and people who loved you, and you hid from them. You hid from them and you died and now you're gone and it's too late."

"They're just saying that stuff online to look good."

"How do you know? You never bothered to talk to them. Even that man, that man who loved you like no other, you drove him away because you wanted to be safe. It's my fault. I should have motivated you more. It doesn't matter anymore."

"Mom, I'm happy. I lived a really good life."

"Did you?"

"I…" Cassandra stopped. She couldn't answer. The truth was somewhere along the way she'd stopped caring. Her mother was right. She'd distracted herself and began to see other people as disposable stories for her to tell, and nothing had mattered to her at all.

And now she was dead and the people who had been rooting for her all along had come out not out of obligation but because of loss. Or maybe they hadn't. Maybe it was all posturing. Yes, it was all posturing. Nothing to be learned from it at all. Unless. She needed to walk to a lake or something.

"I'll miss you, Cassandra. But I've missed you for a decade now."

"Goodbye mother."

Cassandra made a slow, three day return to her home and sat down beside her laptop in her living room. Death had reminded her she wanted to be alive. Perhaps for the first time since. Since. Since. She turned to her laptop for the first time in a week and saw a message.

"Oh man. Now Walton Simmons is dead too. Terrible year for all of us. He was the best friend a guy could ask for. See you in the next one, brother."

She hadn't spoken to Walton for more than a few minutes while he was alive, but she remembered his goofy smile. His legs too big for his body. His John Cleese gait. He was a nice guy growing up and judging by his profile had gone on to be a good man. Charity work, small business owner, happy family man, dead. Really dead. Not Cassandra dead. Dead dead. Cassandra felt a tear form in her left eye and her fingers found the keyboard.

"So sad to hear this. Walton was always a highlight in any class we had together, and I wish we'd have spent more time talking growing up. Sorry for your loss. Seems like he did some amazing things."

<u>After These Messages</u>

Eventually, they ran out of things to sell. Technology had reached its apex. Fashion, art, gastronomy could advance no further. Surveys based on a multitude of algorithms revealed that every single possible consumer left on Earth was already resigned to their buying habits, their identity, their preferences and there was no changing their minds. War was a phantom to all but the eldest citizen, so conscription and armament were nothing more than an old ghost story. The wealth hoarders, praise be upon them, had hoarded everything they could. 90% of all jobs were performed by a single high-speed CPU. There was a sudden lull in the market, too many people and nothing to sell them. What ever could we do?

'Well?' asked Vernon Bleak. He stood at a slight tilt in front of the hi-def 3D projector. The rest of the marketing department had no idea. Their career was one of the few the AI had no inclination of doing itself. 'What's the point in selling people things they don't need?' the AI had asked many years earlier. And yet, despite their status and their importance, they were facing irrelevancy. Their midnight clock was at 11:59. If they didn't find a client soon, they would join soldiers, bankers, the entire working class, lawyers, and actresses over twenty-five as a poignant footnote in an unread history book.

People were so short-sighted, buying so much that the world no longer needed advertising departments. Typical selfish humans.

Bleak's department was one of the last bastions of the glorious world of marketing, and they refused to surrender so peacefully. But what could they sell? And to whom? Vernon's underlings looked up through hollow, pleading eyes. Vernon smiled.

'Guys, I'm happy to announce we just opened an account with The KYF Foundation!'

Orgasmic applause from the staff, at least a few quite literally. Vernon had saved them again. Not since the in-utero campaign to persuade babies to skip the breast milk had such good news been delivered.

'What's The KYF Foundation? I'm not going to tell you, but I will show you. I've secretly drawn up some commercials as a jumping off point for all of us to work on. Bon appetit!'

He gestured at the ceiling-mounted camera for the lights to dim. The euphoric nattering the surrounded him dissipated, replaced first by jarring shh sounds and then by muted excitement.

SMASH CUT:

EXT. COUNTRY ROAD, NIGHT

High octane music plays as an expensive car winds its way up a hill. A solitary mansion awaits him, brightly lit against a dark world.

                          MAN
                         (VO)
        What do you get the man who has everything?

The car pulls into the gravel driveway. We can smell the opulence. Close up on the driver's door as it opens. The driver is a handsome former model turned actor in his early forties. He walks to the front door and turns to face the camera.

                          MAN
                     It's simple:

              INT. MANSION, NIGHT

His abode is all the more extravagant inside. Walls are covered in suits of armour, rare paint-ings, Roman pillars. The floor is marble and pure gold. At the foot of a massive winding staircase his doting and beautiful children await. Their loyal butler appears from under the stairs and

presents the man of the house with a semi-auto-
matic tactical shotgun

                        MAN
               You murder your family.

The camera pans to a close up of a roaring fire-
place as the man executes his entire family before
turning the gun on himself.

                     SEXY LADY
                       (VO)
      When there's nothing else left for a man of your
           calibre to do, murder your family.

                                          FADE TO:

EXT. BEACH, DAWN

A former model turned actor in his mid-twenties
and his inoffensively attractive and ethnically
ambiguous girlfriend are walking hand in hand down
an exotic beach. Twee ukulele music plays as a
raspy falsetto sings a public domain song.

MONTAGE: Beach, coffee shop, rooftop bar, front
row at a concert, a walk in the woods. This young
and attractive couple are in love.

INT. DEFRAGMENTATION STATION

Finally, the couple walk into the defragmentation
chamber (coming soon) ready for their next adventure. A scientist ushers them under the deatomis-
ing ray in the middle of the room, and they, the

couple, share a passionate kiss as they are oblit-
erated. Camera follows their particles ascending
into space. Freeze-frame of the galaxy in all its
majesty, the two lovers' atoms intertwined to form
the company logo.

CAPTION: ENDING IN DEVELOPMENT

                    SEXY LADY VOICE
                   (VO, impassioned)
        You come from stardust. Isn't it time you went
                         back?

CAPTION: OR:

                    SEXY LADY VOICE
                   (VO, whispering)
        Together forever. Only with the defragmentation
                        chamber.

CAPTION: OR OR::

                    SEXY LADY VOICE
                 (VO, confrontational)
        Anyone can get their photo taken outside the
      pyramids. Not everyone gets to explore the infin-
                      ity of space.

                                        SIDE SWIPE TO:

Close up of a failed model turned internet personality as he high fives the camera. They are
recording in their usual recording space, a bedroom or soundproofed office.

Whattup my press gang! How you all doing? It's
your main boy, the memezilla Paul Mark Eccols,
coming at you right quick with a few messages. But
first, hit that like and subscribe button. And
don't forget my merch links down below. And while
you're looking at my sweet merch, guys, why not
consider murdering your entire family, guys? Now
this video we're going to look at how to make
explosives out of objects your mom keeps around
the house, and where to find the most easily
accessible arteries on the human body. But first
guys, here's my new music video. That's right,
y'all, hitting you all up with a surprise jam!
This song is called How to Kill Your Entire Family:

As the generic hip hop intro to a forgettable song began, Vernon mercifully paused the video. The lights came back on. His staff were impressed.

"I hate that last guy, but the kids love him, right? So those were only concept videos. We're going all out with this campaign, and I want to fully explore every available avenue through the algorithms so that everyone is given the right video on the right day on the right device. This contract is worth a lot of money, and if we do it right, we'll go down in the marketing hall of fame. I'm going to need you to form your own teams and focus on the primary targets first - gamers, middle management, single parents, the disenfranchised 18-40 bracket - you know the drill. Yes?'

One of the newer hires had their left hand raised. They stared at Vernon like an insecure shut-in stares at a flirtatious stranger. 'Uh… I don't like it.'

'This project is worth a quarter billion dollars up front, if you think…'

'No, sir, sorry: I just mean that the first video needs a wine glass in the last shot or something. The fire and the gun shots together don't mesh well, according to latest studies. We want the audience to associate murdering their family with relaxation, not hellfire. So wine. Or, or, or, some fine jewellery, a huge television perhaps?'

Vernon pointed at the new hire with newfound appreciation. 'Yes. YES! That's exactly right. Guys, this is why we have these meetings! I need you to really think about the psychology of these adverts because it's imperative that seventy percent of the world's population is killed within the next twelve months.'

Three months later, and Vernon Bleak was enjoying an old film on his hyper-real television. He could only watch antique DVDs from before his company had added mandatory hyper-relevant adverts into every frame. He was breaking the law doing this. It was illegal to look at any work of art without watching at least three commercials every two minutes.

He felt a presence by the door leading out into the corridor. His son, Fallopian, was standing in the doorway.

'Oh, hi, sport. Dad's just watching some old movies. Don't tell mom.'

Fallopian didn't respond.

Vernon looked closer at his son. Fallopian's cola sponsored pyjamas were smeared with something. If more than ten percent of his clothing was obstructed, Vernon would be fined by the advertising council.

'Sport?'

Vernon paused the old movie and crawled over to his son. His sleeves were covered in fresh blood, but Vernon couldn't see the source until he looked down the hallway into the master bedroom. The room was illuminated by an overturned lampshade, fresh arterial spray decorated the wall beside the king-sized bed. The last few spurts from his dying wife's heart sputtered with increasing irregularity down onto the linoleum floor as she gargled for help.

Only then did Vernon notice the kitchen knife.

'Uh? Sport?

Vernon smiled despite himself as the blade came down.

The campaign was a huge success.

An Editorial

<u>Y'all, contrary to popular opinion we fo sho spoke like this at my elite private school, aight?</u>

<u>By</u>___________________

Aw lawdy, they at it again. Yall know me by now, Chloe Wilco-Parsnip MBA. Some of yall might know me from my extensive work as senior financial coordinator at my father's multinational company, but most yall muh'fkers know me from my fire AF feminist Twitter account @___________. If you new to my yard right here, I got some bad news for yall, cuz: some people done been complaining about use of certain lexicon recently. Check it, some haters really do be saying I be appropriating various minority cultures in an attempt to both gain social capital and mask the fact I have an estimated net worth of $10 million, not counting my inevitable inheritance once mi papi kicks it.

But yall, think about this for a second:

How can I be offensively mimicking linguistic, colloquial trends when we all talked like this at my elite private school?

Mm-hm, Felicia. So, I'm about to end this quejarse right quick: because I've got to asset strip some struggling Bronx business this afternoon before kicking it in Williamsburg this evening with my gorgeous queens. Yasssssss.

Your ears did not fail you. My elite private school just so happened to be full of jargon and idiolectic eccentricities, yall, and the fact they resemble "current popular slang used in impoverished, black, queer communities" or whatevs, is a complete coincidence. N'est pas?

Yasss, I remember when our civics teach Bretland Oakley PHD would stand in from of class and say 'Ooooh-eeee, yall fissin to live up to yalls potential up in here today.' Or when the principal, Reginald Featherbottom PHD, would announce over our cutting-edge speaker system 'Órale, vato, we be having a free period this la tarde in honour of our school's patron saint Ayn Rand.' This is, was, and always will be how we speak up at my elite private school.

In a lot of ways, I am inclined to remember the drama last year over my debut novel, Las Familia, a heart wrenching tale of a Mexican immigrant, an Auschwitz survivor, and a strong-ass black woman coming together to solve a murder, all while that blasted patriarchy tries to stop them. Do you even remember that storm in the proverbial teacup, yall? Because I sure as heck do, foshizzle.

I remember running to my publisher in tears. 'Tia,' I cried, 'All these ratched ass looking ass people be all up in my grill, yo, saying I'm exploiting a growing need for inclusion and diversity for my own personal ends while simultaneously I be being part of the problem, guvnor, whattup-witdat?'

I came into her Lower Manhattan office convinced I was a fraud. Maybe I was just another cog in an imperialist, capitalist, white supremacist machine, maybe I was just using feminism and an array of regional dialects in an attempt to cover up my own complicit nature in these harrowing times. But yall, I was wrong about that. Mi tia, she be done gone look at me all flummoxed and she say:

'Mio dio, Chloe, how could these trifling ass haters be talking all this shit about you? You really do be talking like you be talking on Twitter and in your bestselling novel, because that is *exactly how everyone talked at your elite private school in New Hampshire.*'

She was right, of course. I wiped the tears from my huevos, signed the seven-figure book deal, and joined her for mimosas at an exclusive restaurant. By the time the evening came, and I was buying up properties in Harlem as part of a property development side hustle, I had already forgotten about those cruel words.

And so, today, looking at all the broke-ass, busted-ass fools complaining about me in their editorials and blogs or whatevs, I am choosing to ignore these critiques, regardless of how pressing, relevant, or accurate they are. Instead, I am going to think of mi tia, my fanbase of affluent white suburbanites, and the struggle of being a woman in these trying times. Most importantly, I am going to think back to my days at my elite private school where it was popping off almost all of the time, and we really do be speaking in this pastiche of a vernacular.

And if this hasn't convinced yall to forgive me, let me ask yall this: who does this criticism really benefit? You might think it opens up a debate on the commodification of cultures for fun and profit while simultaneously maintaining the status quo, but hark, no. It actually helps rich white men. I know. I was shocked too when I just said that just now. So, who do we really want to run this country? Disgusting rich white men? Or successful rich white feminists who really do be talking like this, ya feel me? There are no other options.

In closing, to reiterate for yall, we definitely talk like this at my elite private school and if you disagree, you're censoring me and also hate women.

__________'s second novel, Slavery Was Bad, is a harrowing account of a slave girl who was saved by a hard-working and progressive landlady who teaches her the true meaning of freedom. Pre-order now. When she is not writing novels and running her business, __________ is a proud dog mama and member of the Columbia Board of Directors. We out. Peace.

The Market of Ideas

Walt waited outside the window of the Vargas family's living room. He watched with narrow, unblinking eyes as the Vargas boy bounced in his chair drawing pictures of superheroes and villains. The child was singing, but Walt could only hear the tinny reverberations through the glass. He hoped the child's song fell under fair use for two reasons: 1) He wanted to buy the rights to the song, and 2) He didn't want his first meeting with the Vargas family to involve a lawsuit. No, suing a family the first time you met them never made a good impression, and while he would own them in due time, it was best if they came to him willingly.

When the boy had finished his fifth drawing, all circles and lines and blues and reds, Walt pressed his skeletal ring finger against the doorbell and waited. The echoes from behind the glass changed in an instant, with the muted sounds of television and singing replaced by banging and shuffling. Soon the door was open and Esmeralda Vargas, the mother, opened the door.

"Ye… oh," she said. She knew in an instant who Walt was, her chest all but crumpling in on itself as she staggered backwards. "Hello," she whispered.

"Mrs Vargas," Walt replied, his voice a calculated baritone, "Your son turned six yesterday, is that right?"

"Y-yes, but I don't see what that has to do with anything."

"Oh, but you do, Mrs Vargas. I will need to look at his drawings."

"They're all his," a man's voice called from upstairs.

"Yes," Esmeralda agreed, "He knows only to draw his own creations."

"The Company will decide if that's the case." A smile wrinkled Walt's timeless face, his obsidian eyes looked into Esmeralda's. "I'm not here on a copyright search; I'm here to secure intellectual property for my employers."

Esmeralda nodded. "Come this way."

The boy had stopped drawing as was depositing his daily credits into his toy box. Walt crouched beside him, revealing credits of his own. The boy looked up at him, terrified by all but the tokens in the man's hand. With the speed of a pickpocket, the boy snatched the tokens and placed them into the slot beside his action figures. A faint his and a whirr of an outdated hard drive as the protective glass opened.

"You have acquired the playtime rights for… WOLFMAN… and… HUMAN FLAME… for… THREE HOURS. Your playtime rights will cease in… THREE HOURS… at which point you will be breaking international copyright law and The Company will pursue legal action to the full extent of the law," the toy box said in a playful, singsong voice an automaton could have. A jingle played as the toys were ejected out of their spots. The boy grabbed them and began running around his table.

Walt stood up and scanned the drawings. They were good. More importantly, they were original ideas. This would please The Company which would please Walt. He noticed Esmeralda lingering in the doorframe.

"Are they good?"

"Yes, Mrs Vargas, they are very good. I feel we will be able to make a developmental deal for your boy pending an investigation of his past behaviours."

"Past behaviours? He's six years old."

"Even so, it would look bad for The Company if he did something untoward."

"He doesn't even say bad words. We've been very careful around him."

"The Company will decide if that is true. I will personally overlook the fact he was humming Clare De Lune while I was outside as a show of sincerity and support. We love these drawings."

A set of feet stomped down the stairs. Mr Vargas appeared beside his wife. It was clear he had been hiding from a confrontation he could not win. "Clare De Lune is public domain, sir."

"We bought the public domain last year, Mr Vargas. But do not concern yourself with that, as I have granted your household performative rights for all music for the next six months on the proviso your son signs a developmental deal with The Company this time next week."

Esmeralda tried to stifle her smile. Singing again, for the first time in years. She hadn't been able to afford a good song since before her son was born. Her husband, Rufus, was less impressed.

"You want to buy our son's imagination," he said.

Esmeralda stopped thinking of the songs she could sing and looked at her son. "Will he still be able to draw his characters if he's on a developmental deal?"

Walt smiled. "As long as they're new characters. Of course, we'll own them after he draws them too."

Walt sat at the table and spread the boy's drawings out. The boy placed his figures on the floor and sat beside the man. His parents stood motionless in the doorway, arms folded, breath shallow, faces betraying every emotion they were feeling.

"What is this guy?" said Walt.

"That is blood killer death explorer," said the boy.

"I see. Does he have any powers?"

"He has lasers and bombs."

"Interesting. But we already have a Blood Death Killer Explorer in our catalogue and wouldn't want to presume to confuse our audience. Perhaps you could come up with another name?"

The boy looked at him with a vacant stare.

"We'll have some of the boys in marketing figure out the branding, lad, don't worry too much about it. Now this yellow ball guy, what's he like?"

"Oh, that's yellow ball guy. He can turn into a car."

"A car? Would it perhaps be possible if he could turn into something more saleable like candy instead? Just a big bag of affordable candy available at all of The Company's affiliate stores. Could you imagine that?"

"Uh… sure," the boy giggled.

Mr and Mrs Vargas watched for almost an hour as Walt and their son discussed the nuances of the characters on the table. They had never seen their child so engaged.

"You have… TWO HOURS… of playtime rights remaining," said the toy box.

Walt scooped a handful of credits from his pocket and placed them on the boy's lap.

In the evening with their child in bed, Esmeralda and Rufus sat on their couch and scanned their television. Walt had given them a sachet of credits for the television and they would be able to acquire one-time performance rights for some of their favourite shows without having to sit through a commercial break every five minutes. With the credits, they would only have to endure ten minutes of commercials for every show they watched. They didn't know what to watch first. Such uninterrupted television had become alien to them.

"I don't know how I feel about this," said Esmeralda, her finger hovering over the OK button on the remote.

"Yeah, I didn't think you liked this show after the first season."

"I don't remember if I liked it or not. And must have watched it fifty times. But I'm not talking about that. The boy. Do we really want to sign a developmental deal?"

"We don't have a choice, really. The Company always gets their developmental deals. Remember the Cathcart kid?"

She did remember the Cathcart kid. They'd wanted to keep all their ideas for themselves, so The Company created similar characters and sued the child for copyright infringement. The whole Cathcart family were little more than a folktale now, spoken in hushed tones in crowded bars or as a warning to unimaginative children. The Cathcart Family: The Movie was scheduled for a Halloween release. The Company also owned the trademark for Halloween.

They selected a sitcom about a plucky woman and a sarcastic woman and an ambiguous everything male friend. Then there was a knock at the door. They weren't used to visitors.

It was a handful of neighbours all huddled together. Some of them had brought manuscripts in brown paper envelopes. Others had painting wrapped in canvas, CDs covered in marker scrawl, USB drives. They looked at Esmeralda with watery eyes. She had never spoken to a single one of them.

"We hear the boy has a developmental deal," said one of the neighbours.

"Yes," said Esmeralda.

"We, uh, we just wanted to come in and share an idea with you guys if that's OK."

Esmeralda looked at the reflection of the television on the nearby mirror. It was illegal to pause a show once it had started. But the sadness, the shame, the desperation in her neighbours' eyes pulled at her conscience like a magnet.

"Make it quick, please, we're going to bed soon."

The neighbours stood in single file in the living room. They'd rehearsed what they were going to say but, in the moment, had forgotten just what it was they wanted. Rufus looked beyond them to the television. The plucky girl and the sarcastic girl were dating the same guy but didn't know it. Esmeralda tried to look demure despite not knowing what the word demure meant.

"We, ah," one of the neighbours spoke up, "This community is not represented well on television and we don't mean to impose on your child and all, but we were hoping maybe you could get our ideas to The Company. We don't care if they know we did them, you can pretend it was all the boy if you want. It's just..."

Another neighbour inched forward. "We just want to be heard. You know how it is. All that talk of inclusion The Company gives us doesn't mean much of anything. So..." they put their manuscript on the coffee table. "This is a very personal story about my experiences. We all have them, and we all want to be heard. But it's hard to get heard when we know The Company has reached its quota for everything this year."

"Please," said a third neighbour, "This would mean a lot to us. Even if it means we can never own our stories. Just so long as someone knows how we feel."

Esmeralda nodded along. Rufus has stopped watching the television.
"We'll do it," one of them said.

Walt arrived as promised at the start of the following month. The boy had drawn more characters in anticipation: Skull Chief Blood Destroyer; Green Boy Farting Robot; Shark Killer Rocket Man; Ninja Sword Laser Breath; Colin. His parents had rewritten the ideas of their neighbours so they appeared more like something a six-year-old would create. Walt noticed the pile waiting for him at the table.

"That's quite the stack of work," he said.

"Oh," said Esmeralda, "Yes, once he realised what a developmental deal meant for him, all he could do was create things."

"Fascinating. Just the sort of ambition we're after at The Company. Who knows, he could make it as one of us when he is older?"

Esmeralda tried to mask her shudder by reaching for a nearby sweater.

"I will begin, then," said Walt, handing Esmeralda a special voucher for uninterrupted television. "Please if you could all just sit there while I read that would be most helpful. Why not watch this year's remake of one of our old cartoons?"

"Which one is that?"

"Any of them."

The Vargas family sat watching the animation, trying not to think of how vivid and imaginative the original had been. The boy was exhausted, having spent his credits on a huge quantity of candy. He rolled around the couch between his parents who were busy pretending not to listen to Walt.

Walt had brought with him a tape recorder he would speak into while he read through the ample material. Never once did he wonder how a child had created so much. Perhaps he didn't care.

"Good strong female lead in this story, but strong females should be attractive and have no flaws," he said after one manuscript.

"This story is diverse and inclusive but mentions class too much. If we made all the characters rich, this could definitely sell well in overseas markets," after another.

"A perfect superhero story this world is after. The only change I would make is to replace the vague anti-government rhetoric with a pro-government one. Perhaps include an agent or politician to counteract what is clearly a misguided view of the world."

"This is diverse but too diverse. Needs a solid anchor to ensure we don't lose money in middle America and Australia."

"No one in this demographic has ever endured adversity as described in this otherwise delightful tale. Replace the main character with desirable at-risk youth after studying current trends. Possible award winner in the making."

And so on. The Vargas family sat in silence. The adults in shame, having betrayed the wishes of their neighbours. The boy because he had fallen asleep upside down.

Finally, Walt stood up. His smile took up his entire face. "And all these are his or were given to him voluntarily?"

"Yes," said Esmeralda.

"We will need to change a lot of the material around. But I don't imagine a six-year-old understands how the real-world works, so we won't hold it against him. Congratulations, your son has just made you rich."

©©©

For six months, the Vargas family hid in their homes. They could not meet their neighbours' eyes or acknowledge what had happened. Nobody came to visit them to ask about their manuscripts. Walt was the only person they spoke to.

But the stories were all turned into films and they were paid for their troubles and decided to move just as soon as they could. There was a community for families with children on developmental deals. Esmeralda didn't want to move, her son even less, but living with the guilt was worse.

There was a knock on the door.

One of their neighbours stood with a handful of unused moving boxes. They smiled as Esmeralda answered the door. "These are for you, heard you're moving," they said.

"Why thank you," she replied. A pause, then a cathartic release. "I'm sorry."

"What for, hon?"

"Your story. What they did to it. I'm sorry we let that happen."

The neighbour laughed. "Are you kidding? My story made it to the cinemas. Sure, maybe I was mad at all the changes they made originally, but when I thought about it a little more it was so much better. You reach a much bigger audience when you take out all that guff I included about oppression and how working people should unite."

"I liked your original draft."

The neighbour waved her off. "Please, I helped make The Company a billion. Even if they will never know it, I'm glad to have helped. Anyway, good luck with your move. Tell Rufus I said hi."

Far from alleviating Esmeralda's feelings of shame, the neighbour's happiness made her all the more guilty. The Company had done it again. And now. And now…

Her train of thought was interrupted as Walt appeared at the front door.

"Hello, Mrs Vargas," he said, "I see your neighbours are happy for you. I am too."

"Yes, it's all been a bit of a whirlwind."

"Very good. I came here today to thank you. We know your son didn't write all those stories, but since we own the rights now it doesn't matter."

Esmeralda stepped back, eyes scanning for her family. To warn them. To run. "Am I in trouble?"

"Not at all, Mrs Vargas. On the contrary. We have been so busy looking for children we forgot about everyone else. You've presented a great opportunity for us to find a whole slew of fresh ideas we can rebrand and give The Company shine to."

"They're people's stories."

"No, Mrs Vargas, they are our stories now. And we will do with them as needed to tell our truth to the world. Thank you, your son has made men like me a lot of money."

Behind Walt, a hundred limos parked up along the street. Out of each, two men exactly like Walt exited. They hovered, these replica Walts, floating with haughty grace toward each door on the street. They brought with them contracts, briefcases, pockets full of credits. They would buy every idea on the street and wash them clean and the street would thank them in return.

<u>Netflix Pitches #1</u>

- An angry ghost must solve its own murder. The only problem? Ghosts aren't real.

- Something something murder, blah blah, sleepy town, yadda yadda, all is not what it seems.

- A popular public domain character is reimagined as an underdeveloped minority and/or woman in a cynical attempt to generate free publicity while also missing the opportunity to make any sort of real and lasting social commentary.

- A real national tragedy that befell some third world country or another, as told through the eyes of someone who was slightly famous in the 90s like Kevin Sorbo or something. Anyone actually from that country will be cast as either a vapid love interest or a drug dealer, because that's all those countries are good for, beyond the obvious exploitation of their national tragedies for hastily produced soap drama.

- A tall, beautiful, popular, intelligent, rich, funny, witty, stunningly attractive high schooler with low self-esteem struggles in high school for some reason, and we're all expected to care for some inane reason. They end up dating the slightly less attractive of the two models pursuing them because, I don't know, some shit about personalities or something.

- A raucous, edgy comedy special where a multi-millionaire celebrity is given two hours of free publicity to make fun of the LGBT+ community and complain about how oppressed and censored they, the porcelain-toothed, grinning jester who owns a ranch, are.

- A banal retread of a cancelled cult favourite about three years after people stopped asking for it. Dead characters brought back based on popularity and scripts read like erotic fan fiction, and something about, uhhhhhhh, time travel or multiple dimensions.

- Inspired superhero movie where a group of underdeveloped and attractive actors must find a series of McGuffins with no real stakes or drama or urgency or character development, and maybe there's, like, a laser shooting up into the sky and everything is colour-corrected to the point it makes the viewer's eyes hurt.

- Show about racism written by two white members of the intelligentsia where all the racists are poor, cartoonish stereotypes of hard-working individuals and all of the cops are friendly and progressive except for one who gets his comeuppance, and ultimately it's the cool, neoliberal millionaires (none of whom are racist) who wind up saving the day, because you can't give minorities too much autonomy, or they'll get ideas above their station.

- A shark with legs and a talking orangutan ride around the country in a motorbike and solve crimes in what appears to only be one coastal town but is actually rural Louisiana, honest.

- Celebrities talk about how coronavirus ruined their lives and how everyone who died should consider themselves lucky when compared to what the celebrities must have endured

- The child of a celebrity or producer or whatever writes and stars in some trashy, irony-laden mess with a dull, gimmicky premise. Appears alongside a handful of their friends who are also related to celebrities and producers. No need to worry about editing the first draft, the media will fawn over it despite the weak performances and poor plotting.

- Just 90 minutes of straight up porn. Maybe every episode we can watch a bunch of struggling LA writers watch the porn with their partners and make a bunch of mawkish gags about pubic hair or something.

- Three strangers discover to their horror and delight that they're not actually strangers at all but then slowly rediscover they are strangers as they sober up.

- Really gritty drama that gets ruined because all the cast insist on eating with their mouths open and oh my god please stop doing that, I'm turning it off.

- Depressingly realistic melodrama by a failed playwright turned TV writer who swears they don't hate women but will nevertheless die alone.

Sometimes, you leave pages blank and feel guilty because of the trees.

But the trees are already dead.

Thank you for your sacrifice.

A Jim for her Pam

Q:

A: No, at the time what was important was she swiped right. A hundred other women didn't that week. Who am I kidding, that week? I mean that day. Her profile was funny enough. One too many TV references, same as any other lady in that age range, but there was some genuine stuff in there too. Which is rare. I guess a guy with five matches in a year shouldn't be whining about rare, though, eh?

Anyway, back when we were just talking on messenger, nothing seemed too off. Not really. Again, a few too many "oh this is exactly like in season three of The Office yadda yadda," but nothing the brain downstairs couldn't put up with. Right? It was those pictures, though, man. That's what should've tipped me off. Something about her profile pictures. Now, I know, I know, but you're wrong, OK? Wrong. I'm not a shallow guy. It was her face, man, her wide-eyed glare, her plastic looking face. It was like a mask or something. Just this, like, surprised looking face trying to smile. In every picture. Exactly the same.

That's what I said. Her face was exactly the same in every picture. Her body though? Man. But that face. I still see it standing over me.

Q:

A: What?

Q:

A: Oh, well, at the time, you know how it is. I was lonely. And plus, there's so many damned filters out there these days it's hard to guess what's real and what's a photoshop of whatever. I was thinking maybe her face was like some deepfake or one of her modelling photos or something. Because there was definitely something off about it. No way a woman that young and that healthy gets her face stuck like… huh? No, that's what I'm saying. I thought she just sucked at photoshop like those fitness models. You know the ones who curve their hips just so and suddenly there's like five leaning towers of whatever the fuck behind them? Like that.

Just her face instead of her ass.

I mean, what? Every time I match with someone with that stupid dog face thingy, I'm supposed to assume they're half dog? I don't think so. I mean… No, yeah, I get the joke. Just because I'm shallow doesn't mean I want you going around calling every woman I ever met a bitch, though, yeah? OK. So.

But besides the face thing, which honestly, at the time, I just put down to bad photography, there wasn't much to dislike about the girl. She was flirtatious but not, you know, trashy with it. Funny. Humble. Always answered her messages when she read them. You know how sometimes you can just tell they've read the message but they're waiting to reply. Like it's a game. Just a big fucking game to them. Like that? She never did that. She'd reply and reply and reply and then, if she was doing something, she'd like me know. Picture that in today's dating scene. "Yeah, got your message but I'm going to bed now." Who does that? No one. Not no more they don't. Or so I hear.

There was one thing. I mean besides the photos. Which I thought less and less of the more she started insinuating certain stuff. There was, look, I mentioned it before, but some of these chicks really love The Office. The US one, though. With the… yeah, yeah. So, you have to get used to these references you might not pick up otherwise because you haven't binge watched the entire show six times like… Yeah, no, I'm calm, man. I'm calm.

This chick, and get this, her real name WAS Pam, this chick loved The Office. I mean *Loved* it. Capital L and everything. I didn't pick up on how much she was into it at first but the more we talked. I mean….. We'd be subtly flirting. Late night shit, you know, "oh, think I might have to take you into the bath with me it's getting so late ha-ha just kidding" type stuff. Goofball shit. But then sometimes out of right field she'd come out with "ha, that's more of a Toby thing to say," or whatever. Maybe two or three times a day. No rhyme or reason.

Yes, it was a little annoying. I wouldn't say troubling. Just annoying. You know that kid with a new hobby in school who wouldn't shut up about it? It was like that. If the kid with the new hobby was of legal age, interested in you sexually, and had the body of a direct to DVD actress. What I mean is, this was the furthest I'd got with a woman online for… since, since you know. Don't make me say her name, man. You know who. That's to say I wasn't too perturbed by her favourite TV show. Really, compared to some of the stuff these women like, it was a relief actually. No MLM stuff, no vaguely fascistic politics, no three other boyfriends she lives with back home. It was just a TV show. How bad can being obsessed with a TV show be? I thought.

Everyone says they're obsessed with something. Everyone.

Q:

A: So, the days turn into a few weeks and her messages get a little more sparse and I just know. *This is it.* My shot at her is almost over. So, I do it. I ask her out. Right then and there. No coercion, mid-conversation, while I'm on break at work. Of course, then I have to wait until the end of the shift to see the answer, which sucked. You know that little lump of hot dread that floats deep in your gut when you're expecting the worst? And I mean the worst for any-thing, an argument online, a "we need to talk" text, that unshakeable sense that something bad is going to happen even when it doesn't?

But yeah, obviously she said yes. We wouldn't be having this conversation if she didn't say yes. Do you think I'd… no, you're right. Sorry.

We meet up at this place, Picky Wick, or something. Some bar. Down in Woodlands. It was a little out of the way for me, but I think we've established I was a little lonely. What's that? Well what's the difference between horny and lonely? Really? There's a lot of overlap, isn't there. You know there was a time in my twenties I'd take girls home just to. No, forget it.

Fine. I took them home just so I wouldn't have to sleep alone. I'd single out the most easy looking target, take her home if I was lucky, and just fall asleep with my arms around her. Some of them digged it. I don't know. It's how I met… never mind. But anyway, Pam.

I get to the bar before her. It's a pretty nice spot all told, not too many people, no one trying to DJ on the jukebox, bartender actually seems to like other human beings. The markings of a good bar, in my opinion. I just sit at the bar for a bit. Sip a beer. Talk to the bartender.

It's only after thirty minutes that I start to wonder where she is.

I asked the bartender, I says, "Hey, I don't guess you've seen a woman in here? Name is Pam. We were supposed to be drinking right now."

The bartender kind of just laughed and nodded over to the dark back corner behind a pool table. She's been there the whole time. I can tell she recognised me, even, because she's just sitting there in the shadows, the light from the pool table giving away her outline, reflecting her teeth a little. She looked hot.

Q:

A: No, obviously I couldn't see anything. She was sitting in the shadows. But the… the silhouette or whatever was a nice shape and her teeth were all there and sometimes you can just tell someone is hot.

But so, I buy two more drinks and saunter over there. I can hear her giggling. A sort of breathy laugh, like it wasn't her own. Like people who think they're Irish lilt the end of their sentences when they're drinking, you know? A nice laugh, but a fake out. It came out of her whole face. Even close up I couldn't get a good look at her, but I said, "What's so funny?"

And she said, "Oh, nothing. Just I was watching a TV show before I came here, and this is exactly like a scene from that show."

I sat down beside her. At that point I could see the sort of black pool glow of her eyes. They didn't seem to want to blink. I sipped my beer, and said "Oh yeah, what show?"

"The Office of course."

So that should have been a clue. She'd been sitting there in the corner all that time trying to create a scene from The Office. But I rewatched the whole show after the… after the… you know. And I don't think I saw that scene one time in any of the episodes.

And this other thing. When she spoke she had this really hokey accent. I couldn't tell if it was a put on or if she'd just travelled a lot. Who am I to judge, right? I only speak English and maybe habla dos palabras en Espania. But it was definitely noticeable. You could tell she'd taken classes or watched a bunch of videos, because every now and then her real voice would slip out.

But really, we had a very nice chat there in the dark. It sort of made things more intimate, because all I could really look at was the glow of her lips, the contours of her upper body, those eyes. I'd never felt so connected to anyone in such a short amount of time. All in the eye contact, I guess. It felt… It felt like a first night with a woman with the lights off, you know what I mean?

Just a raw physical connection and nothing else to go on but lust or passion or whatever you want to call it.

So, of course, Dutch courage kicks in, I have a pulsing… I have an er… I'm in the mood to take her home, everything is shaping up nicely. So I say, "Say, I think they're trying to close up for the night, maybe we could head back to my place?"

She laughed. "Oh, Jim," she said. "I live just down the street, why don't we go to mine?" And her hand kind of reached out and squeezed my thigh and it had been so long since I'd talked to a woman my whole body spasmed there for a moment, but I don't think she noticed, because by the time I'd finished my little episode she was halfway to the exit. And I have to say, I know it's weird saying someone's shadow looked hot, but you should have seen her from behind.

I caught up with her outside and we barely talked. We're walking along, she's holding my hand, nuzzling my neck. Got me feeling like a thirteen-year-old who has discovered girls but not the internet, if you catch my drift.

Q:

A: … Yeah, I mean obviously I couldn't see her all that well. It was dark, the lights were dim, the roads empty, I was tipsy, she had her lips on my neck… take your pick for the reasons I didn't notice until we got back to her place.

And she was right about that, too, she did live near the bar. Her home was kind of empty. Like she didn't know what to put inside it. No point of reference or whatever. And she tells me to make myself comfortable in the living room while she gets changed. So I do. Lights are out in the hallway, so I have to sort of feel my way into where I think the TV is. Lights out in there too, but I fumble around and grab the remote. She didn't have cable or anything, just a connection to a Blu-Ray player. Which, I mean, good for her, right? Cut those cables. And guess what's in the player? The Office. It's one of the later seasons. But I leave it on, hoping it might score some points or something.

It's only when my eyes adjust to the gleam of the television that I start how she's decorated her walls. Lots of pictures. Printed out at a library or something. They're all scans and photoshops of the chick from the Office. Then, and I don't know why it took me so long to make the connection, but I figure it out. She looks just like Pam. No, my date Pam, not the... they look a lot alike. Except, of course, that can't be right.

And then it dawns on me all far too late to do anything about it that I haven't actually seen my date Pam's face all night.

Q:

A: Yeah, it's easy to say you would have realised it now, after the fact, but you weren't there, were you? You have no idea what it's like to be so lonely and in need for human connection. And besides, I'm thinking to myself, in that dark room, so what? She wants to look a bit more like a TV character. Or maybe she's getting work done to look less like her, you know? Can you imagine how living in LA would be if you looked like someone famous? You couldn't even order a coffee without some schlub trying to give you their screenplay or business card or...

Yes, I know we're not talking about struggling actors here. What I mean was my brain was going one eighty in a fifty five with the doors open and I have so many questions and dawning moments of clarity all wrapped up in those seconds, I couldn't hear her as she snuck up beside me.

I saw her face then for the first time, she was just like in the pictures. Unblinking, sad eyes, a desperate and concrete smile etched on her face. She was Pam all right. I realised what she must have gone through to look like that, and I leaned in to kiss her. And then she sunk the needle into my neck, and everything went black for a bit.

I must have woken up a few times while she was doing it. I could vaguely feel my arms and legs bound in tight restraints. Sort of numb and lightheaded, like after you've just fainted. You barely recognise your own limbs. I couldn't feel my face, but I could feel cold air blowing on parts of my head that shouldn't be able to feel cold air. I couldn't move. I'd catch glimpses of her looking down at me, looking so happy. She was wearing a surgeon's garb and it was smeared with blood....

Yes, probably my blood. I mean, I know now she had her own Roy there for a bit, but I doubt she only had the one set of scrubs. Pam's not like that.

And then... she left me down in the basement for about six months. For the first few weeks I was drugged up and numb to my own anger. Shocked, I guess. I could feel the sutures on my face, the faint tracklines that shouldn't be there. Everything itched but I had to stop scratching because I kept drawing blood and she didn't like that.

She'd come down every few hours and we'd talk. Mainly she'd make me read scripts she'd already prepared, and we'd recreate these scenes. Great scenes, by the way, and that was all pretty nice. I think I fell in love with her pretty quickly, if I'm honest. Some people say it was the Stockholm Syndrome, but she's just such a nice woman, Pam is. Don't tell her I said this, but she's even nicer than the one on the show. Please don't tell her I said that.

I don't even mind that she cut up my face. Honestly, I was always more of a Dwight anyway, so the fact she saw the Jim in me and dug it out of me, that just shows the kind of woman she is. Who does that, you know? She saw the man I could be and not the man I was. Online dating, man, there's not a lot of that around anymore.

That's what she's done for me. Pam has really brought out my inner Jim. I'm funnier, more assertive, confident. She's going to let me have sex with her soon, if I've got the episodes down just right.

But anyways, yes, to answer your question, I am very interested in a career in paper sales

<u>I'm Going Through Some Stuff</u>

- 55 -

Dear Agnes:

Sorry for the delay in returning a final draft. I agree with the editor's note in that the first chapter of a book should set the tone, and I see how *in medias res* is perhaps best suited for more visual forms of creative expression. Maybe when you get us a film deal, huh?

Again, apologies for waiting until zero hour to finish the rewrite. I don't want to get too personal here for a litany of reasons, but I worked as hard and as quickly as I could under the circumstances. Hopefully we can secure a publication date and move on without lives.

Cordially yours,

Oscar Sumpter

I:
Hot is the Star which
Burns Above Tumbleweed

Nothing grew in the town of Tumbleweed. The wrath of the Old Gods had salted the earth eons before man dared defy their will. A stolid, carrion town between two worlds. If it ever rained, as seldom it did, the avaricious dust of the Earth would drink with insatiable thirst and yield nothing in return. A land of sand and rock and heat unrelenting. High above the town and desert expanses an eternal ball of flaming fury spun ever onward toward nothing. Nothing. Nothing: what I meant to you.

The new sheriff rode the bone white and limpid road into town on his pale horse, black suit turned grey by the wind. He surveyed his new domain with squinting eyes, brow glimmering with sweat and grease and agua. How much agua he had wasted on his sun-kissed and scarred forehead.

A caravan of supply carts slowed his progress and he found himself behind a wagon filled with canvas sacks of grains and starches. Wood splintered and broken like a promise. In the shadows of the wagon he could she the gem-stone glare of watchful eyes looking over him. Eyes cold and detached and sparkling, like the eyes of a woman who has found someone else but cannot find the courage to tell her partner of six years.

The slow, plodding approach seemed to go on forever. As was often the case, the sheriff found. The three days ride between towns would last a single blink while the last half mile would take an eternity.

The wagons stopped outside the general store and the sheriff's trot became a canter once more. Riding through the town, he took in his new domain. The last sheriff one of several men still waiting in their beechwood coffins for the preacher to arrive. Two moustachioed banditos hired to stand outside the bank. A single house loomed on the crested ridge of a small cliff. At the end on the long, straight stretch of dirt was the sheriff's new home and station. His castle.

As he clopped on toward shelter and a fresh bed, he glanced over at the saloon, a place more lively than anywhere in a hundred miles. A raucous mob of miners sang merrily inside. Outside the front door stood a woman. She looked like an Anne or an Annabelle or an Anna. Annie maybe. She was beautiful, and smart, and funny, but on a fundamental level it was clear she was a narcissist, a coward, a delusional and treacherous and cruel succubus. She exchanged a brief glance with the sheriff and the attraction was instant and palpable. But she was going to take the next stagecoach out of town to "start living her true life for herself and not be held back by others" even though those others probably paid for her rent and groceries for three years while she tried to make it as a photographer without any training. The woman left the saloon and the town and would never, not in a million years, be seen again.

As the sheriff and his horse made it to his new abode, a deputy skittered out from behind a wall. His long, skeletal arms flapped in the breeze, his vulture-like face gave as close a proximity to a smile as it could muster. Well, gosh, said the deputy, weren't expecting y'all 'til sundown.

I guess I rode fast, then.

Guess you did, sheriff. I'm deputy Howitzer.

The sheriff spat. How come you ain't the sheriff, deputy Howitzer?

On account of my bad eye and gimpy leg. Y'ain't be seeing me chasin' no robber any time soon, I reckon.

I reckon not. The sheriff let out a slight laugh. The laugh of a new friend. Not the laugh of a self-absorbed woman realising her boyfriend of six years is crying. Crying because his heart lays broken in the dirt while she makes vapid Snaps for her friends about crying men who can't satisfy her or something. Something like that. You know what I mean? I bet you do.

They entered the sheriff's station. Old relics of former sheriff's littered the wall. Torn wanted posters. A bullet hole hung like a halo above a chair at a desk. To the left, the cells, all empty. To the right, his new bedroom, as squalid as the last. Had the sheets been changed since the last sheriff died?

Well, I'll leave ya'll to it, boss, the deputy said.

All right.

The sheriff sat on the chair his predecessor had died on and leaned back. He peered through the station's one window and looked out into the town. A ramshackle mix of buildings all built against the rules of nature. How had Tumbleweed been allowed to exist? Beyond the buildings, the white sand of desert plain. Beyond that, a sky of imponderable blue. And not just any blue, but the shade that was your favourite colour. A shade someone would memo-rise right down to the hexadecimal code because they loved you so much they would engrave every small piece of you onto their soul if they could. Because every muon of their being loved you completely. Could the same be said form Jake or James or John or whatever his effete, WASPish name is love you with that much attention to the innocuous minutiae of your existence? Would he love your little kernels of information or would he remember only your favourite drink and possess some vague, abstract idea of your menstrual cycle? Not borne out of love but out of self-serving needs and carnal lust? And the dead trees on the plains signalled another failed harvest.

I don't know how many more years of failure this sound can take, a voice said flatly.

A man in red flannel and pre-ripped denim jeans stood by the door. He had naval tattoos but couldn't swim and had grown a big bushy beard in lieu of a personality. He couldn't even name five The Beatles songs but wore a John Lennon shirt under his ironed, unwrinkled plaid. Him? That guy? Really? Him? That guy? Well just fine, I guess.

Can I help you, mister…

Please, called me Jamie, all my mates do.

Mates. James was clearly from Butte, Montana but had affected Australian slang in an effort to appear more interesting.

What can I do you for, Jamie?

I just wanted you to know that I am going to take everything you hold dear.

The hell?

I said, il sont fait un cinematique mon cher. I thought I should introduce myself before the… more simple folk of the town get your ear. I own the reservoir and the mines just outside of town. And yes, you could say I have a small army at my disposal, but any rumours of me trying to drive these good common folk out of the plains is pure horsewash.

I see, I see, said the sheriff.

Jamie leaned forward, scrapping silt off the windowsill. I hope, he said, we can come to an understanding. The last few sheriffs weren't particularly, what's the word, agreeable. Shame they died in such a brutal way.

Now if you're trying to threaten me…

Nothing of the sort. Just a friendly observation. Now if you'll excuse me, I have to go and get my monthly allowance from my rich dad and then perform my bad Sufjan Stevens impersonation in front of ten people at the saloon. That's apparently enough to destroy six years worth of sacrifice and trust.

I'll walk you out.

Oh no, don't you worry, sheriff, I was in here just last week because I'm a toxic delinquent if you'd just open your eyes for a minute. Like I say, though, I owe everything to my rich dad, so I'll never know what true suffering is.

Jamie left the building and let the door slam itself shut. The sheriff sat still and pondered the words he had heard. He took some tobacco from the desk and chewed it. Chewed it and spat it out. Like how someone can treat their closest friend. Chewed up and spat out. Disposable.

For all the talk of equality and respect and communication, in the end the sheriff chewed up the tobacco and stripped it of everything good and pure and real, used it for its own inane stories to share with their fallow and insipid friends, sucked the marrow out completely until all that was left was a broken husk. And that was what really bothered the tobacco. That it was so quickly forgettable. Not a lover, not a friend, not any of the words used to assuage guilt, but something meaningless and replaceable. The tobacco was just a story for a tourist to tell on a rainy day, and nothing in the past six years had meant anything to the sheriff because the sheriff only really cared about themselves. Sure, they liked to pretend they were progressive and hip and empathetic, but they were just another parasite. A solipsistic mess of a human being deriving pleasure through their own id and unconcerned and unmoved by the feelings of those around them. Even those who maybe gave up a film deal on the other side of the country because there was talks of engagements and buying a house and unrealised dreams. And you seemed worth it, Agnes, you really did, not that it matters anymore. And the tobacco sacrificed so much and ended up spat out into the trash can of history like it meant nothing at all. That was the real blow. Not the lie or the cheating. The complete lack of guilt, of responsibility, of owing your partner at least an apology. Isn't that right?

The deputy burst into the room, gun aquiver. Sheriff, come quick, there's a shooting at the bank! We must move fast!

Nothing ever grew in Tumbleweed, but it could certainly die.

<u>Jackie Boy</u>

The door gave in with comparative ease. It had, in all likelihood, been kicked in almost habitually since the mid-sixties thanks to a combination of police raids, break-ins, abusive lovers, and paramedics investigating the smell of rotting flesh, overflowing bathtubs, or the crash-bang-thud-bang-thud song of the ever-popular murder-suicide.

But, despite all that, the frame itself had never been replaced. Landlords in Kings Court would glue everything back together a thousand times before buying something new. They'd replace any missing pieces with scraps of MDF and then paint over it. The entire neighbourhood was like the Ship of Theseus, more a concept than anything real. A gust of wind would obliterate any and all the buildings and no one would miss them.

Which was what Jack was counting on.

Tenants had been given three days to leave. No explanation, no compensation, no refunded security deposit. The owners needed to build something more important than housing for poor folk - a coffee shop, a dog grooming store, a vacant lot. Jack had watched the demolition crew seep the perimeter, but noticed they hadn't bothered to go inside. It wasn't worth the effort. After this finally sweep was when Jack kicked in the door to 110.

It's illuminating to see what people take when they're forced to leave in a hurry. A wall-mounted and massive television had been removed, as had the contents of an elaborate entertainment system. But the bookshelves, photos, potted plants were untouched, left to disintegrate. Still, a few hundred could be earned if Jack could get it out without being noticed. More in the other apartments, he nodded to himself.

There was a pack of cheap beer beside a pleather recliner. Jack sat down, got comfortable, and helped himself. It wasn't as if the owner would miss it; they were never coming back and Jack was never leaving. Holding the beer in one hand, he removed his kit from his jacket with the other.

Jack would've been a year sober on Sunday. They'd have made a big deal out of it at the meetings as they had every other time. 'Big Jack's last second chance,' his sponsor would say. Even as he sat almost horizontally on a stranger's recliner, Jack couldn't verbalize what pushed him to use again. He'd been coping more than usual with a string of strained relationships, removed a third of his financial woes, and even held onto a job past the probationary period for the first time since college.

Maybe it was the dawning realization that this was it: a never-ending fight to be only OK, to survive. It was the clarity of knowing he was livestock; that a million faceless companies would find a million Machiavellian ways to bleed him dry. And, no matter how hard he tried to make it otherwise, his life was essentially predetermined. There was no happy ending for him. This is it. Drinking beer in an illegally-entered apartment and the eternal nagging of self-loathing.

He called his grandma out of habit. In the past, he'd call her up at the start of a binge, meeting her to acquire some cash, hating himself every second he did so. But now, he called her so he had someone to say goodbye to.

'Hello?'

He almost hung up.

'Jackie Boy, is that you?'

'Oh, yeah, hi grandma. How's it going?'

'Oh I'm doing well, Jackie Boy, can't complain.' She paused, having had this conversation a hundred times before. 'I don't have any money this week.'

'No. No, no, no, that's not why I'm calling. Not this time,' he let out a puff of nervous laughter. 'I wanted to let you know I'm flying off to Asia tomorrow. Finally found a good job.'

'Oh, that's lovely, Jackie Boy! That's lovely. Are you going alone?'

Jack tucked the phone into his shoulder as he tied a piece of surgical tubing just above his elbow. 'Uh… no, I'm going with a non-profit. Thought they'd keep me honest.'

'Oh, that's great, I'm glad you finally have people looking out for you. I always thought this place was your downfall. Too many selfish people leading you astray.'

'Well, not for much longer, eh?'

'Yes! Finally. I'm so happy for you.'

In twelve hours, King's court, Jack, and the unread book collection of 110 would no longer exist. Why not be a ghost travelling the world instead of a sad, cautionary tale? It was better for everyone. Jack realized he was staring at his lucky spoon, not talking to the only person who loved him.

'…So, where in Asia?'

'Mm… I land in Shanghai for orientation, but I'll be spending most of my time in Cambodia and Thailand.'

'Wow. You lucky so-and-so. This is a great opportunity, Jackie Boy, I've got a good feeling about this.'

The problem with second chances is you never get back to where you started. Diminishing returns. All that hard, introspective, painfully honest work for an ever-decreasing plateau of normalcy. Eventually, the ebb and flow become interchangeable. Using or not, life outside becomes the same banal constant. It stopped being worth the effort three relapses ago. The brown clump of good stuff balanced in the centre of his lucky spoon.

'So, yeah, granny, I wanted to call and thank you before I go. I don't think the reception is good where I'm going. You're the only person who has always been there for me. Even at my worst. I know I can be…' Jack continued to talk but he could only hear mumbled echoes of his own voice. He was too focused on the needle, fighting a panic attack. He'd never had the nerve for intravenous stuff. It reminded him too much of past suicides, which seemed fitting.

'Oh, Jackie Boy! Don't mention it! Anything for you, my love. You were always one of my favourites.' She laughed. Jack hadn't heard her laugh since he was fifteen. 'Don't tell the others I told you that.'

No more 6AM calls to renege on parental obligations because the bathroom is covered in blood and shit. No more borrowing 50 off Nick to give 30 to Thomas for a few pills. No more taking a beating from Scruggs because you've decided to keep the other 20 for yourself. No more pretending you don't know what happened to the car, or waking up in intensive care with only a police officer for company, or having to cry alone outside a funeral home because everyone inside thinks it's your fault. The lighter took some convincing to work.

'If you'd had more support growing up, Jackie Boy. You were always so talented. I hate that I couldn't have been around more.'

No more living in a world where the only people who call you are debt collectors. No more failing, or letting everyone down, or being acutely aware of your own misdeeds and hating yourself as you do them, compelled by some dark force you can't beat. No more of any of that. Jackie Boy was on his way to Cambodia to feed orphans and build villages, and that was how people were going to remember him. A success story. A fictional success story, but

not the tale of a man as broken as the door of 110, incapable of being anything more than glued together chunks of shrapnel.

'I know you don't believe this, Jackie Boy, but everyone loves you. Even if
it doesn't feel like it. That thing with your dad wasn't your fault. It wasn't your
fault, honey. I hope you forgave yourself.'

Maybe he was crying. He couldn't tell you if he was. The first hit was
always the best.

'I know, mawma, I know. I'll send you a postcard when I get there.'

That was the last thing he remembered.

They never would find his body. When he was finally out of his own way,
he could have the life he should have had if it wasn't for all the troubles and

And and and

    And

And

                    Ddd

And a a aaaaaaa

    And

           And

                   A

        N

                      D

          AND

The View from Above

They looked down on the ruins of Machu Picchu, of Angkor Wat, of Atlantis, savoured the sun as it disappeared behind the pyramids, impossible skylines of futuristic cities never to be realised, ancient Rome. Anything they could imagine projected with ultra-realistic precision across a ring of screens. The true outside - hidden behind glass, lead, wire and concrete -long since irradiated, ash covered, choked by inescapable blankets of toxic smog.

The two of them stood and looked at the changing vistas. Friends long gone but immortalised through deep learning systems sent messages of support while an artificial fanbase of phantoms cheered over a multitude of social media platforms. They had succeeded. According to the charts and graphs projected over the fake windows, their wealth had surpassed all other survivors. A great day.

She had long since forgotten her real name or what she had looked like before the nanomachines could sculpt her to daily specifications. Ideas like success and fame were lost in the haze of the back of her mind. But knowing that they had won was enough for her. The machine in her head told her so. A dead friend's words, tweaked by algorithms and neurological scanners to deliver just the right information, arrived moments before any real introspection could occur.

He knew he was older than her by thirty years. But that age difference had lost all meaning five hundred years earlier. A patchwork of cellular tissue and the latest robotic parts, the only thing he feared was his reflection. The terror would subside in a nanosecond, however, as an unending stream of artificial hormones would regulate everything. Keep him motivated. Sharp. Precise. Anything for the pursuit of more wealth.

They couldn't remember when their chase for profits began. The modulators in their brains wouldn't let them remember anything that wouldn't benefit their happiness or their wealth. No daydreams of lost children or family, no recognition of the consequences of their actions all those centuries prior. All that remained were the swirling mirages on the panes of their penthouse, the climbing graphs and bank balances, the adoration of their preprogramed fanbase who would flood their photos with "wow this is so impressive, hard work works!" and "living the dream! Keep reaching for the stars!"

Neither needed to eat, their inbuilt network did that for them. Just sit back and relax and let the network of regulating devices take care of it. All fun was performative, created on the software of their choosing and projected out into the wastelands for other towers to enjoy. From the safety of their suite, they could dance in palatial ballrooms or hike over mountains with equal ease, both real and not. They thought they were happy.

He had brief synaptic visions of her in her youth and how she looked before her appearance was controlled by computers. Of kissing her. Of celebrating their life and success together. These glimpses lost as fast as found pulled into a writhing sea of half-remembered facts. What were facts? He couldn't remember. All he could remember was that he was successful and that when the white line beamed onto the screens went up it meant they had won.

She had dreams of dreams, a vague sense of dissatisfaction worn into the marrow that no amount of chemical assistance or nano intervention could quite remove. Too numb to acknowledge it, she instead watched in what she thought might be awe as the salt flats of Bolivia gave way to rolling Martian tundra. The machine at the base of her neck told her to enjoy this, so she did. Even as her lips morphed and warped into the mouth of another dead celebrity, she formed what she thought was a smile.

A chime rang out. An incoming call. Monitors raised from the floor to meet the pair at face level then flashed on. One of their friends was calling. Their friend had died when their tower collapsed, but they had left enough data for the machine to reimagine them. "I'm happy for you two," the ghost said, then sputtered back into non-existence, monitors wafting back into the ground.

Happy? It was a word the pair knew but they couldn't remember. Were they happy? They supposed they were. After all, they had all the money in the world. They could change their appearance on a whim. Their body fat was the perfect amount, their intelligence upgradeable and honed, their moods regulated by the machine. Their tower was the highest of all towers and they would live forever. Why wouldn't they be happy?

These were things they would say if they still spoke. Too distracted by the screens and the constant recalibration of chemicals in their brains, they did not feel a need to speak. Adulation and wealth were enough for them. Besides, she and he had run out of new things to talk about centuries earlier, when there was still hope for the world outside.

In the factories below, Uri and hundreds like him worked endlessly. His body modified so that it would never age or tire or die, he stoked the fire of the generator as he had always done. It was his job to keep the fire alive. The gift of his work was eternal life but the cost was debt unending. He would work down there in the factor until the tower collapsed or the sun died. The old Uri was angry and bitter, but all that was gone now, regulated by the machine. He had to keep the fire alive and the tower running efficiently. Forever. He stoked the fire as he had always done. The machine told him he was one of the lucky

Excerpt from an Unfinished Novel

"Rebel Man" Bobby Joe "American Eagle" Freedom-Mcfarland was born Ian Xavier Farsoun-Gerbick to a Jewish Librarian mother and a secular Palestinian immigration lawyer father around thirty years ago. He was voted class clown two years in a row at his private school and was the captain of his Ivy League University's improv troupe X-Rated Yams. After receiving his double major BA in Journalism and Theatre Studies, Ian X moved around the country taking every overpriced improv class he could find until he was discovered in a small storefront theatre. From there he went on to write and occasionally perform for a weekly live television show until he was unceremoniously fired for a pro-feminist sketch that was misinterpreted as patriarchal pro-rape propaganda by a small but vicious number of internet users.

It was after this that Ian became Bobby Joe, a beer-swilling, camo-wearing, tar-chewing good ole boy from down south. A country singer with a heart of gold and a mouth of dirt. He reached critical acclaim with comedy songs such as Fistin' Cousins, Them Jew Crooks and Mooslems, and Chains on the Back of my Pickup. They were, he thought, fairly transparent joke songs about aggressive bigotry, double standards, and a culture's terrifying efforts to dehumanize and murder entire races of people. But, much like his feminist sketch had cost him a lucrative television deal, nobody seemed to get the joke. His song performed most favourably in the communities he was lampooning; Charlton Biggs, noted racist serial killer, requested his song Curb Stomp Fever as his last request on death row; the current president played the first half of his second album without interruption or irony before beginning his end of year speech.

Ian/Bobby Joe really liked money, so he wasn't about to own up to the thing, but he tried to make it obvious to his listeners in increasingly less subtle ways that he hated them. His third album, If I Were An Israeli-Palestinian Comedian Pretending To Be A Redneck, Y'All Would Look Pretty Stupid Right Now, debuted at number one in the charts and stayed there for four months. His single Them Folks was a shoe-in for the Christmas Number one, and his impending suicide by shotgun to the face was guaranteed to solidify his as a demi-god in a culture he was terrified of.

We love God, beer, and guns,
Our blue pickup truck
If you tangle with us
Man, you're shit out of luck
'Cause we're real patriots
Proud and True
Real Patriots
Bleed the RED WHITE AND BLUE

Billy John Liszt sang along, screaming "Red White and Blue" over the speakers at such volume and intensity his already sun-baked face was turning a shade darker than strangulation purple. His sleeveless denim shirt revealing a labyrinth of faded tattoos (designed to give the message "ex-military" without any of the self-sacrifice bullshit that goes along with actually being ex military) and manual labour scars, one hand deathgripping the steering wheel while the other gripped his sixth lite beer of the day. He'd nudge his passenger, Earl, every time Bobby Joe sang something particularly patriotic, splashing beer everywhere in the process.

Billy John was leading a convoy of three trucks to The Docklands. It was their American duty.

We got trucks full of guns,
Bellies full of beer,
Shootin' people dead
If they're illegal, black, or queer
'Cause this is the white man's land
What part of my .44 don't you understand?

Earl had never seen his best-friend and mentor so happy. Billy's emaciated, varicose legs, looking like leftover barbecue ribs being devoured by engorged worms, twitched in anticipation. Billy was the first guy in high school to reach 6'1" and, thanks to a swathe of personality defects, never realized he'd stopped being particularly tall or intimidating around forty years ago.

"Oooh-eeeh, Billy, we're going to get us some looters today!"

"We sure are Earl. Those sonsofbitches. Who do they think they are? They're stealing from hard working Americans like you and me! The president has the right idea. Blow 'em all up!"

Mary Sue and Jimmy Schubert in the truck behind them honked as they spewed coal smoke out of their exhaust.

"Aw shit, look at Mary Sue! Those cyclists didn't like that!"

"Shit, bet they don't even know what coal is!"

"HAHA, they don't even know what fucking, what fucking CARS are man!"

Earl and Billy laughed.

"So Billy? How we going to spot looters? I don't want to shoot anyone what don't deserve it."

"They all looters Earl. If they run they must be guilty of something, so best just to shoot them. Besides, you think anyone is going to miss a couple of dead thugs?"

"I guess not, Billy, I guess not."

"Toss me another beer."

Earl obliged. His face looked like a malfunctioning animatronic gorilla's that had been left out in the sun and then repurposed as a troll once the wax had begin to droop.

"Hey, Billy…"

"Yes Earl."

"Some folks are saying that Rebel Man is a joke."

"Who's saying that?"

"Just people."

"Liberal sheep trying to keep a good man down. He's a patriot."

"But a lot of his songs are explicitly about murdering black people."

"Race don't got nothing to do with it. I don't think he once mentions race."

"I guess maybe those liberals are the real racists."

"If they think thug means black, that's on them, that's what they think, Earl, you're exactly right, their PC culture stops 'em seeing how racist they are."

"See? Could be about anybody."

"Rebel Man" Bobby Joe "American Eagle" Freedom-Mcfarland had read some old aphorism about a clown who tried to warn the theatre it was burning down, only to be met with laughter and applause by an audience who thought he was joking. The world would end to the applause of wits who thought it all a joke. If only it were that simple, Bobby Joe/Ian would write in his journal minutes before his put the barrel in his mouth.

The Ultra-Unified Theory of Everything

Danielle Muon looked out at the rest of the CERN tour group, her right hand hovering over a blank whiteboard as it gripped a non-permanent marker. To her side, the guide, a PHD-having quantum physicist, who stood with their arms crossed, their smirk betraying a yearning for some basic public mockery. Danielle could make out a vague spectrum of feelings from her audience: Schadenfreude, lust, confusion, an eagerness to get back to Geneva while the fountain was still on. It had seemed like such a good idea, only moments earlier, to say she had the answer to everything.

'Well go on, then,' the quantum physicist said, 'Go on and prove it if you really think you know more than everyone here.'

'OK.'

Blocking the board with her frame, Danielle wrote down the theory. Her surrounding peers look on anxiously. And then, she stepped back, presenting the Ultra-Unified Theory of Everything in its entirety:

$$P$$

'There.'

'That's nothing,' the quantum physicist said.

'You just don't understand it.'

A young man in the crowd, who may or may not have known anything, but was at the very least was wearing a Caltech t-shirt, stepped forward. He had fallen in love with Danielle the first time he saw her, thirteen minutes earlier outside the visitor centre. 'Now wait a second, I think I understand. Yes, it's amazing, you've done it.'

Another tourist, an engineer from Calcutta, approached the formula and also remarked on how beautiful it was. 'It's beautiful,' they said. Then a third, a fourth, even a ninth person remarked on the theory's accuracy.

'Everybody back up,' said the quantum physicist, as they nudged the group away from the whiteboard. Fingers gently pressed together in front of their minuscule mouth, they looked the equation up and down.

P

'Ah, yes, I couldn't quite see it properly from over there. And to believe what a huge part my encouragement had on the creation of this… this masterpiece! So elegant. So… revolutionary!'

By the time Danielle returned from Geneva to her small studio apartment in Gillingham she had been heralded as the new Einstein. Better than the new Einstein because she had no connections with either her cousin or communism. In one warm spring afternoon, she had unravelled and unified all the many mysteries of science with a simple stroke of a non-permanent marker. The marker in question had already surfaced on an auctioning site with an initial bid of half a million USD being met and surpassed tenfold within thirty seconds of it being listed.

There was talk of a Nobel Prize. Perhaps the very last one in science, since science had essentially been solved.

By the time Danielle had unpacked her suitcase three weeks later, she had a growing number of suitors, agents, and talent managers vying for her attention. Billionaire geniuses who made their money having other people do all their work wanted desperately to meet her, to have her look at some of their prototypes. Morning, evening, and late night television hosts from around the world wanted to talk to her for exactly three minutes as the third guest of their shows.

There was talk of a film being made. Producers, sensing innumerable awards, wanted her to sign off on the rights to her life for a stylish, taut film. All they'd have to do to ensure awards aplenty, they claimed, was to simply rewrite her entire history, race, sexuality, and mental health. Maybe give her a slight disfigurement so that the beautiful actress playing her would only be a nine, nine 1/2 out of ten.

But there was a much deeper impact on the world beyond fame, love, and financial success for Danielle, because suddenly everyone, everywhere understood everything. And because everyone understood everything, nobody had to explain anything. If people disagreed, and many did, the disagreements revolved entirely around who had misunderstood the glorious, all-encompassing formula.

Understanding string theory, m-theory, dark energy, the third act of Mulholland Drive were now as simple as ABC. 'I understand how fifth-dimensional beings exist,' someone would say, 'because **P**.' It all made sense thanks to the plucky insights of Danielle Muon, the brilliant genius scientist.

Religions, far from fearing such an exquisite equation disproved the very existence of a god, were overjoyed. Not only, they said, did it actually prove their chosen deity's existence, but it also showed just how much harder and more mysteriously their god had been working. Some of the more enterprising religious minds went further and suggested that perhaps it also meant that their regular donations should be quadrupled - an opinion their congregations agreed with without hesitation.

It also proved that God didn't exist to atheists and that God might exist to agnostics.

P proved just about everything else too:

1. It proved that the world was the shape of whatever you wanted it to be;

2. that ghosts and cryptids and aliens were real, even the ones that somehow contradicted the existence of other beings;

3. that parallel universes and time travel and interdimensional beings were very real but we just had to wait on advances in technology is all;

4. that life was just as meaningful or meaningless as everyone had always assumed;

5. that Gary's ex-wife Sharon really did cheat on him back in '02, even if the evidence at the time seemed ironclad.

And so on.

Perhaps conveniently, the governments of the planet realised quite quickly that they desperately needed to spend more money on weapons due to some of the more troubling aspects the equation had implied. What were these troubling aspects? Well, if you understood the equation, you wouldn't need to ask such a stupid question. Some bigger governments, you know the ones, scrapped everything in their budgets besides military spending and their own inflated wages.

Plus, since science was solved, schools were free to cut it from their curriculum. And just to be safe, they also cut humanities and what few arts programs still existed. Students had far more serious things to learn, like how to enlist in the military.

Of course, Danielle was not without her detractors. Porcelain-toothed, leathery pundits, the kind of people with no real convictions or moral inclinations who would have gladly beaten their own parents to death had they been born into a totalitarian regime, insisted that Danielle must have had help coming up with the equation. Surely a man must have helped her with some of the finer aspects of the complex formula. One particularly pundit, completely comfortable in his masculinity, whined for seven hours about the evil that is woman scientists all without finishing so much as one sentence.

Bestselling but intellectually sallow modern philosophers and internet hucksters opined that the theory wasn't even all that special, to begin with, and besides which, they'd collectively arrived at the same conclusion years ago, but just forgot to tell anyone.

Danielle was saddened that even though people acted as if they understood the formula, no real changes were being made. The world was still on fire, as it were. She'd need another formula, one that wouldn't just unify science, but people too.

While the world outside her small Gillingham apartment continued to beg for her to talk, Danielle started work on an even more revolutionary equation. When her many potential agents stood outside and demanded she pick at least one of them, she simply closed the curtains. If a grandstanding, dishonest buffoon challenged her to an online debate, she just stopped checking her phone. If a cadaverous entrepreneur flew their private helicopter onto the roof of the building hoping to copulate, she would make sure her door was locked. Nobody was going to distract her.

The following year, she did indeed win the Nobel Prize in Everything. She also, in a way, won an Oscar for The Troubled Genius Years of Daniel Muon, a contrived, problematic film that vaguely resembled her life if one were to plug their ears and squint at the screen.

'I am so honoured to be up here to accept the Nobel Prize in Everything,' she told the sell out crowd at the Chichester Stadium. 'It has been an interesting year of me, not least of which because of the formula.'

The audience laughed at a joke that didn't exist.

'Yes, the formula seems to have taken on a life of its own. And I wish I could say that's what I wanted to happen, but it's not. You've taken a simple P and used it to justify every petty, worthless opinion you've had. You've ignored real and significant suffering while patting yourselves on the back for pretending to understand something. You've accomplished and offered nothing of worth. And you will be judged for your sins… But there's hope. I have another formula, one I wanted to unveil today to the world so that we might collectively work together toward a better future. If you'll indulge me…'

She looked out at the audience with a blank expression as her old friend, the quantum-physicist-turned-millionaire, pushed a familiar whiteboard onto the stage.

And she wrote.

$$P = \oint \sqrt[3]{\Sigma} \% \text{don't be a douche}$$

Not this page, though.

This page is a dick.

The Bends, or
Rejected Submission #273

Beyond the cracked sidewalk, and the telephone pole with layers of flyers in a rainbow of colours, and the patch of dry brown grass there stood a ten-foot-high concrete block wall, caked with dozens of coats of paint. There was a small shrine at the foot of it, with burnt-out candles and dead flowers and a few soggy teddy bears. One word of graffiti-filled the wall, red letters on a gold background: Rejoice!

A lone poster captioned MISSING fluttered down the street, carried onward by an unrelenting, humid wind. It flew just above the ash-strewn and empty roads, making its way down a dozen similar streets, each a tableau of fading memorials. Ground littered with forgotten mementoes, shattered glass, and dead birds. The town of Lamplight, once an industrious town, rendered a mausoleum for the missing and departed.

Rainbow was oblivious to the outside world as she drove into the heart of Lamplight. Her focus was on the three-by-five pixelated map leading her to the nearest gas station. Eyes only glancing through the windshield to scar for cars and red lights. It was only when a digital sound pinged with increasing tenacity and the car's engine shuddered and died that she was forced to look at her surroundings.

She stepped out the car with a fearlessness reserved for the ignorant. Alarm still chiming inside. For the first time since the interstate, she looked at where the sky should be. A dense, orange-hued and roiling mist had claimed all but twenty feet in any given direction. The homes and businesses either side of her were vacant, broken versions of their former selves. Thick red Xs smeared over makeshift barricades and barriers. Lawns and sidewalks littered with everything from broken bottles and spent shells to picked-through suitcases and torn clothes. *What?*

Not too far along the road was a billboard. SAINT SYMEON'S MINISTRY: ALL WHO SEEK SALVATION WELCOME it claimed. Each step toward the church presented another glimpse of a nightmare. A cannibalised wreck of an old sedan lay on its side, bullet-riddled and stripped of parts. Faint oily draglines visible beneath the silt leading out into the road. The church itself a burnt-out husk, black and skeletal like mummified remains. The salvation of an angry god. No sign of life, but then too no signs of death. A small blessing.

With an urge to run back to the car growing with every step forward, Rainbow tried to visualise her GPS. She should have brought it. Too late for regrets or going backwards. The harder she tried to recall the map the less she could remember, until she could barely visualise her past at all. Vague flashes of memories new and old. A hazy image of drive-through kudzu-enveloped back roads as she… *As she?* Where had she been driving from? To? All but the now at once locked behind a synaptic paywall. Trying to think of anything sent shotgun blasts across each cortex, so she stopped trying to think.

There was a constant clattering of dancing detritus behind her, following her. At times she was convinced someone was stalking her. Plodding footsteps hidden behind the ubiquitous waltz of garbage. Whispering to herself just to hear something new. *It's just the wind. Oh, please Lord. It's just trash.* Her desperate eyes checked the abandoned buildings over and over, both hoping and dreading some sudden change. Anything different. A break in the unending walk toward nothing.

Minutes passed. Or maybe hours. She couldn't tell. For the first and last time since leaving her car, she allowed herself to turn around. Whatever it took to satisfy her growing paranoia. And there it was. Nothing. Dust and ash and mist. Her car, the church, the blocks of locked and derelict buildings all lost in the pulsing cloud.   Appearing from nowhere, zigzagging toward her, a single sheet of paper flew toward her. It wrapped itself around her leg and quivered like a dying butterfly. She picked it up and read. MISSING: UNCLE JOE MUND. GOES BY UNK. BROWN HAIR. TALL. NO REWARD. Setting the paper free, she watched it flap off into oblivion and wished she could follow.

Faded yellow background and dead neon-red bulbs. CASPAR AND SON'S GARAGE AND MECHANICS. The building sat at the corner of a large intersection the way innocent men sit in death row. Resigned to a fate it didn't ask for. The roof above what remained of the pump stations sagged every closer to the ground, front windows shattered, poles bent and rusted through. Anything of use had been stripped away, leaving only dusty outlines like the innocent dead of Nagasaki. Even the two cars parked in the lot outside were little more than frames.

Rainbow entered the garage through the customer entrance. Rows of empty, splintered shelves. Shards of glass piled up outside the freezer section. Dust and oil and blood on the polyurethane floor. Insulation pulled down from above and burnt months ago in the centre of the room, the ceiling naked and cracked. Exposed wires and pipes were torn apart, pieces missing. A single bottle of water ferreted away behind in a man-made hole in the wall. Greedy gulps. Rainbow hadn't realised she was thirsty. Bottle empty all too soon. No other hidden treasure or means of escape in the store. She saw the door to the employee section and entered.

The staff lounge empty, devoid of anything. A find glimmer of light shone through the pried open door revealing nothing but a set of stairs. An upstairs office. Blinds closed. Rainbow climbed up as if pulled by an invisible string. The office fully furnished, illuminated by open windows looking out into the orange haze. She didn't see it at first. Too busy searching the desk, the cabinets, the trashcan. But it was there. Looking at her. First, she noticed the photo of the cherubic man on the desk, happy round head and oversized moustache. Then she saw the wall. Written in something Rainbow refused to guess the origin of. DIOS MIO! DIOS MIO! PORQUE ME HAS DESAMPARADO? Still not it. She found it slumped in the darkest corner of the room, folded over an office chair. Dress pants and a vest. One sock on. That same giant moustache but on a gaunt, emaciated face, body sunk, vanishing under the clothes. Eyes still moving. Looking at Rainbow. Pleading. Unused throat crackled as it tried and failed to speak. And Rainbow ran.

She made it as far as the bottom of the stairs before she began to feel the change. At first little pins and needle sensation across her cheeks, her collarbone. By the time she was outside her hands were beginning to fail. No sooner had she made it to the road than her knees buckled and she walked forward with pathetic lunges as she tried to flee the inescapable. *No. Not like this. Oh please, somebody help me. It was too late.* She flopped onto the ground, rolling onto her back. Beneath her, chucks of glass tried to dig through her clothes as her body made its last spasmodic attempts at movement. Before long her movement stopped. *Hello? Anyone?* No one. She looked up at the hidden sky unable to do much of anything but wait for death to come. Like the man inside the garage, Caspar, the wait might take some time.

As the orange smoke dimmed and gave way to greens and deep blues, Rainbow was resigned to her fate. Often, she would hear a scraping of empty cans or rustling of dead branches, and hope, pray, some ravenous beast was approaching. Anything to end the suffering early. She lay there trying to formulate where she went wrong. Had seeing the dying man in his office prompted her body's rebellion? Or was she doomed the moment she turned off of. There it was again. Off of what? Why had she driven into Lamplight in the first place? Ignoring the thunderous pain in her head, she tried to think of her movements but remembered nothing but empty roads and blue skies. Her entire life stolen from her by her mind.

She must have fallen asleep. If she had woken up with as much of a jolt as her body allowed, it stood to reason she must have dozed off. Must have. She felt none the better for what sleep she had, and she still could not move. Alone in the dark with no ideas and no words. She looked up at pitch blackness and wasn't sure if she was still lying down. Her entire body numb, like the limbs and torso of a stranger. Perhaps she was floating. A noise had woken her up. Behind the scuffles of loose litter and wind, something had growled. Snarled. And was coming closer. Her prayers had been answered and yet now dread filled her heart. She did not want to die limp and blind in the darkness of an alien town. She did not want to die. The snarling didn't care. Padded, clawed feet scuttled over the asphalt behind the garage. Predatory sniffing somewhere nearby, the presence looming in the darkness, approaching, ready to eat. Then a swift breeze. Whatever lurked in the night turned and fled with a squeal and a stillness descended.

Before long a different kind of sound. Rollerblades? Wheels? An unoiled gurney being pushed down the road? *Hello?* Voice already turning into gravel. *Hello, I'm right here, whatever you are. I'm right here.* No reply. She recognised the sound, some locked compartment of her mind remembered. A skateboard. As it made a slow approach the voice of a young boy, almost ready to break, began to speak: *For there were many who failed to see until it was too late, and in their ignorance, they found not strength, not forgiveness, not salvation. Their indecision could not save them. Their lies and the lies of others they had held up as gospel a sure sign of their deserved damnation. This did not happen by accident. Oh no, sir. They asked for.. Huh?* The thud of a foot against the road, skateboard scraping to a stop. She could feel the dim beam of a cheap flashlight travelling across her body.

Are you OK miss? Gargled response trapped in the throat. Her attempts at mumbling stopped at the skateboard scooted forward. *Must have just happened to you, huh?* A figure loomed over her, all but hidden behind the flashlight's glint, a person slowly apparating from behind the glare. A short man. No. A child dressed in altered army fatigues, sleeves severed and hemmed but the rest sagging down to the ground. His face preternaturally worn but still carrying the puffiness of youth. He couldn't have been more than eleven, with his diminutive stature and the three coarse tufts of hair dangling from his chin. *Miss, everything is going to be just fine. Oh, thank you, Lord. You're going to survive, you should thank Him.* Rainbow tried to point at the garage, at the vanishing man inside, to gesture at the beast hidden in the periphery. She felt her index finger twitch for all her effort. Her throat rattled with phlegmatic uselessness and her head spun only figuratively. The boy pushed her onto her side and with a foot pressed down on his board he tugged at her prone body once, twice, three times until she was balanced. He removed bungee cables from his jacket. Tied her down. *Miss, I promise you from here on out you're going to be safe.*

From her position, she could see only the back of the boy, his drooping rucksack, the upper edges of tall, ruined buildings, that thick pulsating mass of nothing where the sky should be. The boy talked incessantly about three things; the Bible in a way only someone who had never read it could, Fun Time, the place they were headed, and the fact that everything was going to be just fine, oh yes ma'am. *It must have been some three years back since His Judgement came to town. But you're in safe, reliable hands now.* His skateboard breezed onto a smoother surface, the swirling abyss above becoming a ceiling, what sounded like a wind-up record player warbled scratched old songs and the pattering of tiny feet slapped the ground. *Fun Time.* She was, it seemed, in a wide, tall room illuminated by flickering candlelight. Children had gathered around her just out of sight. They sounded happy to see her.

A young girl's voice broke through the chatter with forced authority. *Wow. Long-time since we found one of these.* The boy stepped in front of her and faced his audience. *Yes, and just in time too. Something almost got her.* An argument erupted without warning as Rainbow looked up at the pirouetting amber shadows on the ceiling. A difference of opinion as to just what exactly should be done with the rescued Rainbow first. Some wanted to get her changed, savouring the chance to dress and feed an adult. Others were excited to show her their many inventions. Rainbow wanted more than ever to know what was going on or at least to be able to speak, to move, to sleep. How she regretted those wasted days she assumed she once enjoyed.

After a considerable time, the children decided their best option would be to give Rainbow a tour of Fun Time. It seemed a bit of a waste of time to Rainbow, all things considered, but she was not in the position to speak up. She was, however, in the position to be shoved around with ease by tiny bare feet. They softly kicked the skateboard down uneven, varnished wood. The preacher kid served as a guide. *This is the pantry we keep all the food. This is the new church. The old church is--And this is the toy room. Everyone gets two toys at a time but you probably don't need to worry about that. We all sleep in here for safety. Not sure where we're going to put you. I'll have someone fix you a bed. Oh, and this is our piece of resistance.* Rainbow was hoisted without warning onto a deck chair. It was one of many chairs hanging from chains, connected to metal arms and cogs. A young boy began to pedal a nearby bike and Rainbow could see the entire room as the chairs made their slow revolution. She recognised the building as being a repurposed skating rink or basketball court. The children watched her prone body spin around with as close to smiles as their cherub faces could muster. They were starved of a lot of things.

When the ride ended, she was lifted again. The kid slid her body onto a soft pile of clothing among the boxes in the garage. He pulled an old coat over the top, creating a cave that emanated the sweetness of old ladies who frequently powdered themselves -- a light rose motif that played ironically well in the deep recesses of Rainbow's ancestral brain. The pizza kid lifted her head to help her lap water from a hubcap. He broke bits of pepperoni and crust into bite-sized pieces and left them where her tongue could reach them. Much later, she heard him practising his orations like songs. Like monks chanting in the distance, they were a comfort.

Her tongue refused to leave the warm confines of her mouth. She lay there alternating between trying to reach the cold pizza - how the pit of her stomach bubbled like an unattended pan of water - and attempting to hum in unison with the kid's voice. No luck on either front. With nothing else to do, she tried to sleep. Perhaps the morning would bring with it her strength, or else she would wake as if from nightmare far from the cursed city of Lamplight in a bed of her own making.

Her efforts were brief, no sooner had her lungs found the rhythmic pace of drifting away than a scrape of metal pierced the silence of the room with tooth-shattering abruptness. The rusted garage door was being methodically lifted from the outside. Hidden behind the screech of old metal she could all but hear whispers. A sloshing wind of almost-words revealing their true identity as speech only when an articulate P or slurred SH escaped a mouth.

From the safety of her downy cave, she could do nothing but watch as long, steel-toed legs made soft, slow strides toward the main building. Muted monosyllabic expectorations from out of frame as unseen arms flapped and gestured unknowable plans. She wanted to scream *Someone's coming, someone's coming, you have to flee, get out of here* with every inch of her body, down the core of her very essence. All her mouth could form as warning was a pathetic and damp *pshtrurpher* just dim enough to be ignored by the interlopers. The final set of feet - she hoped the final pair - lingered above her sanctuary, poised to probe inside. She could see white wingtips picot toward her, a tentative look at the clothes pile.

And then the screaming started. Wingtips ran off to help his compatriots. Children begged for help, for half-remembered mothers, as tables, tinned food, wood all clattered to the floor. The thudding of a hundred feet or more. Barked growls from scratched older voices, pleas from younger ones. Rainbow in her hiding spot tried to thrash about, to overcome in an instant her paralysis as the heavy footsteps of adult men returned to the garage, bringing with them children who, only hours before, had giggled and smiled, now screaming mucus-filled protests.

Metal doors squeaked open and slammed shut somewhere outside, steel cages rattled the moment they were locked. The men returned alone in search of more children. Rainbow could feel small lakes of saltwater materialise above her eyes still at war with her inactivity. Blinded by tears, all she could do was listen to the yelling, the begging, the children reduce in numbers as the onslaught reached its finale. She lay there praying to anything that would listen for the strength to move until the last child, dragged by their feet, disappeared through the garage. A half dozen trucks revealed themselves with diesel growls and drove away. A guilty, hollow silence descended.

The will to move was all the stronger. If she could just will herself upright she could save the children. Negotiate with the men somehow. She must have something they would want. Her eyes spun upward and she strained to refind her feet, her hands, some small part of her body. If she could reclaim a finger she could reclaim her whole hand, her arms, and drag herself out into the darkness to somehow save the children. If. Somehow. The words of someone who has already lost.

What passed for daylight came five sleepless hours later. The honey glow of the misty outside world poured over the shadows and boxes revealing an overturned floor covered in useless blue tokens, rolls of peach paper tickets, beheaded remnants of fairground prizes. Rainbow lay there dazed, only snapping into focus when the dripping water she heard in the main room began to get louder. Not droplets at all, no, the methodical tip-toeing of a child making their cautious return to the garage. The child lingered at the door for what could have been hours. Rainbow tried to call out again. *Psthluphrer.*

You're still here at least. One small miracle. Did you at least - no, how could you? It's not safe for us here any more. Sorry, I lied to you. The preacher kid pulled the cave apart with a weak, accidental reluctance. His sooty face was marked with a labyrinthine layer of snail trails running down from his eyes and nose. His clothes more torn than they had been, knuckles scraped and red and bruised. She tried to smile at him. *We knew this would happen one day. Come on, we'll get you somewhere safe and then... I don't know. Another miracle.* The child fell to his knees and made a furtive, sobbing prayer to an invisible protector.

They were on the road again, Rainbow bound tightly to her skateboard. It was a sombre, silent walk, with only the wind, the whirring of plastic wheels, and the clanking of litter to occupy her ears. The kid walked as if exsanguinated, plodding robotically toward a new hiding place. LAKEVIEW MOTEL in faded yellow and red. Doors boarded up of missing, windows painted black of replaced by tape and plastic. The door numbers had all been removed and placed in a pile beside the reception. Rainbow was placed next to a shattered vending machine while the child entered the manager's office.

Alone outside again, Rainbow felt overwhelmed with anxiety, her powerlessness exacerbating her worry. A maelstrom of woe was forming in her limp, useless body. Inside, she could hear keys jingling and falling to the ground, the rustling of papers, the shushing of moving furniture. She meditated on the child's diligence until it was dimmed by a fresh sound. Two sets of boots walking into the motel parking lot. *What a thing to just leave lying around* a stranger nudged her stomach with his filthy heel. *Lots of things it's good for, though.* A sickening laugh. Two.

The kid rushed outside. Not with anger or fear in his eyes, but shame. Shame that possessed his entire body as he stood by Rainbow's feet. *Here you go,* he said. *Now give me what I want.* The two men peered down at Rainbow revealing their toothless, sunken faces, eyes bloodshot and yellow, hair oil caked and unkempt. They eyeballed Rainbow as if she were a prize to be won, one they were worthy of. The child looked only at his feet.

Yeah, we'll take her, one of the men said after some consideration. The child looked up with a reluctant smile. *So I get them back, my friends? That was the deal.* The men laughed, one slapping the child's face with such force that he landed on Rainbow. For a moment she enjoyed the warmth of another human being for the first time in what felt like her entire life. The child lay there sobbing. *We don't make deal with brats* a man said *and if you don't like it then do something about it.* The two men pulled the rope attached to the skateboard and dragged Rainbow behind them. Without realising it, her arms had wrapped around her weeping betrayer. *Plshhuh* she whispered.

Before long they were outside a disused factory, wooden boards and pallets still stacked outside for a workday never to come. The kid was pulled off Rainbow, her arms once again limp, and dragged off in resolute silence. Untied, touched, examined by coarse hands and desperate eyes, Rainbow was picked up by the hips and tossed over the shoulders of a burly, tattooed man, the stench of his unwashed body permeating the air as violently as his lunges toward the steel stairs. His friends cheered in support. Rainbow could see only the back of her carrier while they clanged quickly up the perforated steps. With a sudden snap, she landed onto a rough bed. An office transformed into a boudoir by and for men. The muscled thug stood above her with twitching eyes and fingers which formed and unformed fists as if squeezing an invisible ball. He crouched on the bed beside her.

He spoke, his voice more gentle than any Rainbow could remember. His eyes tried to form tears but had forgotten how years ago. *Listen, I am supposed to rape you now. It would be so easy. You didn't even flinch when I said that word. You're stuck here. Just like I am. This wasn't… It wasn't supposed to be like this. This was our reckoning. Ours. But we were the ones saved. Perhaps this is the true punishment. To become beasts before you.* He looked up at the ceiling, the words had gained the weight of his soul and so had trouble escaping. *I'm not going to hurt you, lady. I can't do this any more. I'm not a good person. But I want to be, oh yes, I want to be. Can you save us? Can you save us all? Or is it too late?*

He sat stolid and mute at the foot of the bed, a watchdog. The door would knock but no one would enter. When night fell he stood in silence and walked to the door. Stopping with a hand on the handle he turned. *I won't lock this. If you can. Try.* He left the room and was greeted by whistles and cheers from those below.

Rainbow blinked. Down in the bowels of the factory, she could hear a roaring voice, murmurs of agreement. She knew if she stayed her next visitor would not be as entrenched in guilt. Without realising it, her legs began to flop. While she lay mournful and resolved her body once again had other plans. A sudden rising sensation and she could she the rusted, battered walls of her prison. She was standing. She tried to look around, to move her body, but it had its idea. Still a captive of her own body she watched from the confines of her skull as her limbs moved to the door.

From the platform up above she could see the Old Church. Fifty haggard men sat on oil drums and beams. The children clung to the side of cages. Severed limbs and broken bodies hung from the ceiling on iron chains. A molten fire behind a makeshift pulpit. Standing over the other men, an older, raven-beaked man in wingtip shoes was leading the congregation in prayer. It stopped. He gestured over at the cages and began to speak.

Can we not see now that these children were not out future. Our future was taken from us. And without a future to speak of, the good Lord decided to take the present from us as a gift to end our suffering. But our suffering, OUR suffering is a constant. You feel it, don't you, brothers? The impenetrable blackness invading our souls. These demons aren't a future we want, no sir, and as long as they all shall live we are doomed to this purgatory. Is it not time, my brothers? Is it not time we reclaim the lives they stole from us?

The men, riled up as they were, sat still, unable to bring themselves to the cages. Their preacher continued to talk, to plead with them. Rainbow watched and tried to think of ways to help. No solution. Her limbs, her wayward body began to move again, carrying her out of the factory and out into the darkness.

She walked despite herself until the factory was an amber glow behind her. Despite pleas and protestations, her body ignored her. It wouldn't, couldn't turn around, seeking instead an unknown escape. *Please*, she whispered to herself. *We have to at least try.* Her legs buckled but continued their march to oblivion. She closed her mind's eye and tried to think. An image appeared. A small child, not one from Fun Time. Her child? Was she a mother? The plodding of her feet stopped, her body turned and ran back to the factory.

The sermon had finished and the followers of the Old Church were finding their feet and their willingness to kill. Standing above them, the preacher was frothing at the mouth and barking orders. *Get them! Open their cages and purge them all!* The men floundered, confronted as they were by their barbarity. While the shuffled toward murder, Rainbow clung to the shadows and made her way to the back of the stage.

You know this is the only way, and you choose now to worry? You fools! We must burn the demons and reclaim our lives. The preacher slammed his fists against his metal podium and gestured at the children. Among them, the boy was whispering a sermon of his own. His friends joined hands and bowed their heads while the first group of men found their way to the cage door.

Rainbow could feel the heat coming behind her. The furnace was hotter than the fifth circle of hell. Scrambling at the debris beneath the stage, she pulled out a mop handle and sunk it into the flame. With a burning staff, she turned to the podium and pressed the fire against the preacher's clothes. He lit up in an instant and ran howling past his followers and out into the blank night.

The men, all fifty of them, stood transfixed by what they had seen. Some found the strength to leave the factory, the tattooed man among them. Whether to search for their burning leader or to disappear, Rainbow did not know. Those who stayed stood motionless, their anger turned inward. As Rainbow appeared from behind the podium and walked to the cages, they parted. Some fell limp to the floor, others found seats or walls to lean against.

Opening the cages, the children made a tentative exit. The adult men could not look at them let along thrash out against them. The preacher child, Rainbow's rescuer and betray, was the last to leave his cell. He surveyed his congregation, free again, and turned to face Rainbow.

I did not think you'd come for us. I did not think you would walk again. Sorry for treating you like that. Can you forgive me? Rainbow made to nod but her head continued far beyond where it should have stopped and she saw herself falling face-first to the ground, her body a hollow and disused puppet once again. Small trickles of blood ran down her nose. Through the forest of children's feet, she could see the adult men all succumbing to the same pull of Judgement. Down they fell. One after another, until all adults in the factory, lay prone and vulnerable on the ground. Some tried to form desperate pleas but their voices had already escaped them, their fates decided in an instant by an unknowable hand.

The children tugged on Rainbow's arms, turned her face up, pulled her over the bloated, shallow-breathing bodies who littered the Old Church. She could hear the heels of her shoes scrape against the uneven floor. She had almost forgotten she was wearing shoes. Almost forgot everything. What she did know was that the malevolent and dense clouds overhead had made a slight retreat. The town of Lamplight, what she could see of it, seemed more real. Settled. The air seemed still and noiseless and a slither of sunlight was working its way through the pea soup clouds. She'd forgotten about the sun.

They dragged her onto a pallet jack and jugged at it until the wheels broke through the rust and began to spin. A parade through the city. A city she had never seen before and never would again. Through the doors of abandoned schools and libraries, she could make out the shadows of inquisitive children making their way to the barricades, watching her from the safety of darkness. She felt her lips twitch into a smile. As they made their way through the streets, the preacher child began to yell in a booming voice.

Come ye and hear, the Old Church is no more, the spreader of lies has met his end and his followers lie flapping in the breeze. We have been liberated by this stranger, whose own life is forfeit. Join me if not in person then in spirit with the promise we shall not forget this woman's sacrifice. Even as we prepare her for her final voyage, we rejoice in her humility, selflessness, and meekness. Amen.

Without protest or fear, Rainbow was lowered into a canoe by the children. They surrounded her with happy faces, eyes glistening in the faint slither of sunlight. There were times, she knew, where the uncertainty of her fate would have killed her right that instant. But laying there in the canoe, weak waves rocking it like a cradle, she felt nothing. A past long robbed of her, limbs and mouth, too. The story of her life a book unread and tossed in the fire. Her options were limited, her future out of her hands, all possibilities grim and unhappy and forced upon her. She was resigned to the possibility there may be something waiting beyond the mirrored horizon. *Thank you,* the boy said, looking down on her one last time. They pushed her over the bedrock and out into the current where nature itself took control and pulled her away from the land.

Rainbow drifted out into the still waters and looked back at the children already turning away from her and returning to the town. Lamplight stood behind them, the mist temporarily lifted, revealing a scarred and battered town. The boat rocked gently while invisible forces pulled it away from the town, the children, the mist. In time, night and fog and bad intentions would return. In time, she would be lost to the waters for eternity. But at that moment, that crystal clear moment. *Hope.*

<u>Netflix Pitches #2</u>

(Note: by including these suggestions in a fiction anthology they are both at once simultaneously legally binding and protected by satire and parody laws at the same time. As such, should any of these ideas appear on ANY online streaming platform, the producers of said programming will be legally pursued, sued, and threatened to the fullest extent of the law. Conversely, should any of these ideas already be in development, this is all just a joke, so you can't sue us. But we will sue you. Please give us money.)

- An anthropomorphic shit farts and burps with its grotesque friends for fifteen minutes a pop, accompanied by the grating din of repetitive music and public domain sound effects. This is for children. Why the fuck would you force children to watch this shit unless you have something insidious planned? Also, the anthropomorphic shit falls in love with a sassy, independent female shit because god forbid a kid's show about sentient faeces didn't also try to placate tired, depressed mothers who would have otherwise written lengthy letters of complaint about why sentient, living shit needs female representation, even though shit by itself in inherently feminine to begin with and... too far? But yes, three living turds and a puddle of sick get into wacky adventures and ruin another generation of toddlers.

- Wait for a small independent group of driven, un-connected artists to create something and then throw a bunch of money both at your legal department and at the inevitable sterile clone of their idea, mindlessly ripping off their content and stripping the original concept of all nuance and heart and style just so you can make an extra buck in merchandise sales. You monsters.

- Melissa McCarthy does some zany improv about her puckered asshole for two hours. Directed by Paul Feig.

- A group of rich, successful actresses decide which rapists deserve to be banned from Hollywood and which it's fine to work with — even defend publicly — all while rampant sexual abuse in multiple low-paying industries remains both ongoing and ignored.

- Angry adult men cry about things that are made for children instead of making any sort of contribution to society at all.
- The cartoon Visionaries remade so that everyone is gay. Like, really gay. Not in an offensive way. Just super gay, but in a way that hasn't been shown on television before (i.e. three-dimensional humans with both good and bad traits and a propensity for same-sex relationships).
- Queer as Folk remake but everyone is a humourless heterosexual pushing 50 but pretending to still be in their 30s, and they all microbrew and make waitresses uncomfortable and can't dress for shit but genuinely believe they're stylish.
- You're Irrelevant: reality TV show in which the sort of person who abuses people in the service industry or otherwise is a dick (i.e. existentially terrified nobodies projecting outwardly at the defenceless while death makes its slow approach) call each other irrelevant all while the entire universe goes on without caring about them.
- A bleak, unrelentingly depressing and hostile cop show, because that's what we, as a society, need right now, isn't it? To be more depressed, further reminded the police are murderous bastards. Yeah, good one. Maybe we can trigger a bunch of psychological trauma while we're at it. You'd like that, wouldn't you? Your little streaming psy-ops. I see you, I hear you, you bastards.
- A group of delusional, dim-witted, but essentially OK people are tricked into ruining their lives by a faceless pack of sociopathic producers, because fuck those pretty, vacant plebs, right?
- What if phones were actually good and it was the people who were evil?
- A sitcom about a group of people in their late twenties and there's a love triangle and one of the stock characters becomes the most likeable of the bunch and the person who was supposed to be the lead is quickly revealed to be an unlikeable Schlemiel.
- Ageing male actor who probably sold out his friends at least once in his life in a plea deal and has never been in a fight, much less served in the military, is presented as some sort of masculine ideal and basically just whines about kids these days and never develops or learns anything about himself because he's right all the time, but then he gets fired after some allegations surface and replaced by someone equally as annoying.

- Show based on a video game but none of the writers or cast have ever played it and in fact hate video games as a concept, and it really starts to show by episode 3.
- Unasked for all-woman remake of Casablanca that says nothing about anything but still makes a bunch of money.
- Gameshow in which homeless people are forced to hurt themselves for food.
- Gameshow in which struggling parents are tricked into selling their children to the Clinton Foundation.
- Gameshow in which there's no actual gameshow, but we tell everyone there's a gameshow and just watch what happens as they go crazy.
- Just a string of racial slurs repeated every episode so that people will signal boost the show on Twitter and you can generate more views, only for the show to become depressingly popular because we've tried to ignore the root cause of racism, preferring instead to present everything in flowery binary that does nothing to address any of the real problems society is facing. Or something.
- A werewolf who is also a cop must hide his true identity from his partner, who is secretly a swamp creature, while they track down a serial killer (secretly a mummy). No vampires. Can we just avoid vampires for a minute, please?
- A slow-motion credit sequence we'll pretend is deep and people will agree.

The Game Show

"Mr Spate, you're up in ten," the PA whispered.

Douglas Spate nodded, trying not to bother the person applying a fine layer of powder on his face. He stood and followed the assistant into a conjoining room. While the makeup room had been well lit, inviting, a place befitting a nationally syndicated game show, the room they entered was the antithesis: cold, sterile, empty except what looked like a dentist's chair and a man in a biohazard suit. Not what Douglas had expected at all when he signed up. Although, if he was honest with himself, he didn't even really know what the show was, only that is was an experimental new format with a guaranteed minimum pay-out of six figures. Can't say no to that.

"And of course, you read the fine print about this room," said the PA.

"Can't say that I did."

"Of course not. None of you fucking idiots does."

"Should you be talking to me like that?"

"Why not? You won't remember in thirty minutes anyway, you slathering cretin."

Douglas stared at the PA, not sure what they meant.

"If you'd had had the capacity to read the agreement when you applied, you'd know that before going on the show, we gas you. It's non-lethal, but you will forget everything that happens today, you galloping jizz mop."

"Why?"

"NDAs don't really cut it. Plus think of it this way: won't it be fun watching this in six months with no memories of how you did?"

Douglas shrugged, that was a good point. Plus, it would be rude to leave the show a person down.

"You people really need to start reading the fine print," the PA sighed. Disappearing.

Sounds of the room sealing shut as Douglas sat down on the dentist chair. The air was damp, the chair cold and metallic, putting Douglas in mind of his time in the abattoir. As a low hiss of gas being pumped into the room broke the silence, the biohazard man leaned in.

"You won't make it three questions on this show, you soppy tit," he laughed as the room filled with gas. Douglas tried to formulate a retort but suddenly it was the next morning and he was home.

For several weeks, Douglas Spate felt as if he had done something very stupid on the quiz show, but couldn't quite grasp why he felt that way. It was like in his younger days when he would binge drink and blackout, spending the next several days in anxious conniption, not sure of just what he'd said or done, unsure if other's knew more than he did. Sometimes at night, he'd wake up almost visualizing something that had happened at the studio, but by the time he was fully awake, the slither of an idea had long since escaped

His friends and family had no idea what, if anything, he had done on the show, but there was a subtle sense of shame when he would see them, like he had betrayed their trust. Calling the show's producers, he was told it was a very common side effect of the gas they used, and they were trying to find a different way to induce amnesia in their future guests. As he hung up, a small sum of money was deposited into his account by way of apology.

Douglas Spate lost his paranoiac itch over time, unsure if he even appeared on TV. He moved on with his life, proposed to his long-time girlfriend, put down a deposit on a humble cottage on the outskirts of town, and did what he felt a man of his age was supposed to do -- plant roots, figure out what an IRA was, add and then remove hair growth formula to his online shopping cart three times a day. Life was banal and liveable, just as Douglas Spate had always wanted.

3PM the day of the show's début and Douglas had invited all his closest friends and family over to his little cottage to watch. It had taken several hours to rummage up enough chairs for his guests, with the majority of his deckchairs and student living detritus hidden in storage. An unimaginative spread of canned snacks and lightly heated finger food were placed on a tiny table, but the guests cared mostly about the alcohol; not just because of their drinking problems but because there were so few bottles.

Nerves resurfaced. Having no idea how he performed induced a certain amount of dread in Douglas, and the gentle teasing of his nearest and dearest made him worried if he'd perhaps only made it through the first round. It would have been quite embarrassing for him to have invited so many people over for three minutes of television.

The show opened with bombastic music and a title sequence befitting a summer blockbuster. Fading to a shot of the stage, the contestants' silhouettes in the background as the host, a former alternative comedian from two decades ago, walked po-faced into a bright spotlight.

"Hello," the ex-comedian said, hands clasped together in faux sincerity, "Welcome to the first episode of Amnesia. All of the contests here have had their short term memories wiped, and will not remember what happens today." OOHS FROM THE AUDIENCE. "So welcome at home, not just the viewers, but the contestants too!" UNCERTAIN LAUGHTER.

Melodramatic panning swipe of the stage. Douglas appeared for three frames, prompting a familiar nudge from his fiancé. The camera rested on a middle-aged woman, her eyes squinched shut, head bobbing as if she were suffering from an inner ear infection.

Without prompt, she said "Hi, I'm Vicky, but my friends called me Vicky the Slut behind my back. I hate myself. My most recent suicide attempt was last Thursday."

Douglas' guests leaned in, not sure what they had just heard.

Ex-Comedian, "Lovely! Are you ready to play Amnesia, Vicky?"

"Yes," said Vicky.

"Good!" Dramatic Hans Zimmer music. "Question one, Vicky: Dimitar Berbatov last played for which club?"

"Oh, I have no idea. Football was my ex-husband's thing; I prefer rugby."

Close up of the host. "Well, Vicky, if you don't know the answer, you can always answer a personal one instead." SURPRISED/CAJOLED AAHS FROM THE AUDIENCE.

"Go on then," said Vicky, tilting forward as if attempting to sleep on the podium.

The host grinned. "Good choice Vicky, here's your new question: what is the worst thing you've ever done?"

Vicky rolled her eyes back into her skull. She had been drooling. Her eyes opened a fraction and she tried her best to look at the host. "It was August. I was twenty at the time. I'd been up all night hanging out with my old college friends. I didn't mean to push him onto the track, but it just sort of happened. We were the only two people at the station. He... he just lay there on the track, looking at me. I ran before the train got there, but I don't think he made it. The papers the next day said a man had been killed by a train. I doubt that's a coincidence. I know what I did. I think that's why I've been trying to die all this time. I know it is. I didn't even have a reason to push him onto the track; I just did it because I could."

The host nodded at the audience. There was a spattering of stunned applause as a "£10,000!" flashed up on the screen. Douglas' guests were unsure what kind of program they were watching. "What the fuck kind of program are we watching, Doug?" his father asked.

"I don't know," he said. "They pump you full of gas, and I guess this is what happens to you. Truth serum or something."

"You don't have any bad secrets, do you?" Douglas' fiancé asked, pleadingly.

"Nothing this bad. Think I cheated on someone in high school, maybe did some blow a few times? I don't know." He started to feel uneasy.

Vicky was unable to answer the next three of her questions, and instead revealed how she'd sought out an abortion at twenty seven because she didn't think she deserved to enjoy the pleasures of motherhood, that she'd enjoyed a prolonged sexual relationship with her aunt's second husband in her teens, and that her ideal method of suicide would be driving a 1964 Buick Skylark at 120 mph into the NRA headquarters (she had no idea why, but it seemed like a good way to die, and plus she'd get a trip to the US out of it).

"Maybe if you're still around in sixth months, you'll get to do just that!" the host cawed. The audience laughed, having eased into the spectacle.

Douglas Spate's living room was quiet. Nobody had touched the spread on the table, the alcohol had already disappeared, and even the "ah! I saw you on TV" text messages had dried up.

Vicky finally cashed out with £75,000 after she fell asleep on her podium. As she was ushered off the stage by two doctors, the camera swooped majestically once more and landed on a young, gaunt man. Unlike Vicky, he stared blankly at the camera and tilted back as if he couldn't quite read a bill and was trying to adjust his eyesight. "All right? I'm Bryan, my dad's the mayor. That's the important thing: my dad is the mayor. I go to Durham University but I wanted to go to London and be a dancer. But my dad is the mayor so I had to go to Durham. I've never kissed a woman and my favourite smell is fire."

The audience cheered.

"Please to meet you, Bryan!" Said the host, "Where is your dad the mayor of?"

"I don't want to give him the satisfaction of announcing it on television, but you can figure it out in about five seconds if you bother to try."

The mayor's name and location flashed up on the screen.

"Any funny stories about your dad, Bryan?"

"None of them are funny. He touches little children and worships Baphomet."

"Splendid," said the host, winking at the camera. "I think that one was a freebie, but my producer is giving me the go-ahead to award you a prize for that information."

"£1000!!!" flashed on the screen, the audience whistled.

"First question, Bryan, who wrote the following famous song:

"OUT IN THE FIRE
HOLDING YOUR HEART
NEVER FORGIVEN
ALWAYS APART
I CAME TO SEE YOU
ONE SATURDAY NIGHT
AND THAT IS WHY THE EARTH IS BURNING!"

"Is it… um… Barry Manilow?"

"No, Bryan, the answer is that nobody wrote that song because it doesn't exist. Too bad, Bryan, you leave here today with £1000 and a commemorative Amnesia rug!"

The audience applauded as Bryan staggered off the stage.

Douglas looked around. He had not received a commemorative rug, a t-shirt, coffee mug, pendant, pen, tote bag, trophy, or anything with the show's insignia on it. Had he done worse than Bryan?

"I'm just going out to get some more beer," said Douglas' dad, leaving his cottage for the last time.

Douglas and his remaining guests watched in silence for what felt like three hours as contestant after contestant poured the hearts out and answered a terrible combination of personal questions and specialized trivia. Most of the contestants opted to just talk about themselves, although one contestant, a man named Scott, was able to answer five questions in a row before finally revealing that he was a strong proponent of genocide and had been squandering his company's profits on funding extremists all over the world in an attempt to bring about the end days. He left with £50,000 and a warrant for his arrest.

Kathy, from Derby, revealed that she'd been poisoning her mother's food to kill her off and was only able to reach climax when imagining her childhood pony. Mark from Shropshire told the audience that he'd almost set off IEDs in London three times and would probably do it again, that he'd never had consensual sex, and that his biggest fear in life was being caught. Siobhan had anonymously driven her transgendered friend to suicide not out of bigotry but boredom. Cuthbert was stealing money from his church to fund his addiction to smartphone games. Elijah liked to fight minors for cash. Clara had three innocent professors fired under false rape allegations but never told anyone her father, a prominent member of the conservative party, had assaulted her numerous times. Sebastian's biggest secret was that he could talk to cats. Nikita was a bored spy. Serge believed he was in a computer simulation and that nothing mattered.

The spotlight landed on Doug. At home, Doug was confident about his chances, as he'd never done anything as illegal or as brazen as the other contestants. The producers had probably banked on him having a lot of dirty laundry, as he was third from last in the row of contestants. His guests perked up as his face sloshed toward the camera.

"I'm Douglas Spate, I live in Benton, my life is a failure. I'm scared I'll die accomplishing nothing." AWW, SAID THE AUDIENCE.

"Aww," said his mother and fiancé.

The host's upper lip quivered, revealing his sharp, porcelain teeth to the camera.   "Douglas, are you ready to play Amnesia?"

Douglas nodded.

HOST: "The road was frozen," is a line from which novel?

DOUGLAS: Um, Snow Country, by Kawabata?

HOST: Uh, correct! £10,000! Next question: Anatoly Karpov was born in which town?

DOUGLAS: That's… Zlatoust, isn't it?

HOST: … Yeah. £20,000! Are you sure you don't want to answer any personal questions to double your money?

DOUGLAS: Why? So I can wind up like these losers?

HOST: You've got a point. Next question: Multiply General Pico's altitude by its 2010 census population.

DOUGLAS: You're joking?

HOST: Don't know if you've figured it out, but this show is really all about secrets. Right?

AUDIENCE: YEAH!!! WHOOO!!!

DOUGLAS:...

HOST: You can just tell us about your first sexual encounter if you prefer.

AUDIENCE: Oooh!

DOUGLAS: It's 8,121,685... I think.

HOST: Fu... Yes! Correct answer!

The audience gasps and cheers. Douglas's guests equally surprised. Douglas shrugs both on screen and not.

"How did you figure that out?" the increasingly annoyed host asks.

"Doesn't matter. It doesn't mean anything, does it? Nobody is impressed by the mountain of shit I have in my brain. I'm still a loser. I still have a shit job surrounded by a bunch of complete idiots. They think quoting some old guy's podcast makes them enlightened, like they're better than me because they can pretend to have the same opinions as some idiot from Canada. Does my head in. Of course, they'll all get promoted before me."

Douglas at home writhed in his seat. His co-workers slowly inched toward the exit.

On the television, the host can smell blood. Licking his lips he saunters closer to Douglas' podium.

"Do you often feel underappreciated at work, Douglas?"

"Not just at work: everywhere."

The host nods. "How about your family life?"

"They put up with me, but they've never really loved me. All that goes on my older brother. Even though his stupid kids aren't really his and he's been pilfering from everyone's pensions for years. He's an absolute crook, but he gets all the love. Not that I'm surprised. My dad is an alcoholic idiot and I'm pretty sure my mother has Munchausen's or something. And that's just immediate family. I'm embarrassed to even be associated with the rest of them."

Douglas-on-the-screen sways backwards and smiles as if getting something off his chest.

"But why?" the host says, leaning in.

"Because they're stupid and delusional and racist, and between them, they have done not one good thing for the world where they didn't expect something in return. I don't want to associate with bad people."

"But you do?"

"Yeah, they'll all be over at mine watching, expecting me to give them money and food. I'm just as bad as they are because I'm a coward."

"You really think so, Doug?"

"Douglas. Is this a question for the show?"

"No, just curious, Douglas."

"I think being a bad person is bad, being an indifferent person is worse, though."

"And you're indifferent?"

"Yeah. Too much work to be a good person when you're surrounded on all sides by horrible people."

"Sorry to hear that, Dou…"

"You're a horrible person, too. All your old shows were shit and now you're manipulating people for money."

"Well, at least I'll remember this in the morning."

The audience laughed.

"But, Douglas, you must have someone good in your life, a girlfriend or something?"

In the cottage, Douglas' fiancé smiled at him, acknowledging her positive role in his life. The other guests were silently leaving.

"I have a shit girlfriend, to be honest. She's depressed all the time. Boring. Doesn't like anything I do. Doesn't take care of herself any more. She's selfish and egotistical and deluded."

"So why are you with her?"

"Effort. I told you, I'm a coward. So I just stick with what I know. Beats being alone, I guess. I'd hate to be alone. If I had the balls I'd ask out the woman at the cinema, we have a real rapport."

"Might have to work on that fear after this episode airs," the host mugged for the camera. "But shall we get back to the questions?"

The audience cheered. Douglas swayed gently.

"Next question: according to Egyptian mythology, the thumb was a symbol of what?"

And on it went. Douglas-on-the-screen somehow answering impossible questions, revealing both an intelligence and a level of wasted potential that terrified Douglas-on-the-couch. After each question, he'd reveal a bit more about his resentment for those around him, their failures and hand in keeping him down. He spewed bile on each and every person he'd ever met, judging them as inferior, superficial, fake, and boring. It seemed that nobody lived up to Douglas' high standards, least of all Douglas himself. He talked about himself at length on television with such disdain it was as if he was instead talking about the state of modern politics, unchecked capitalism, the history of slavery, or the final episode of Lost.

Finally, his turn ended and Douglas-on-the-screen disappeared forever. Douglas sat on his couch, alone in his empty cottage, his fiancé's possessions already moved out. He felt numb.

His phone buzzed. It was an alert from his bank; seven figures had been deposited into his account.

He continued to watch the game show, not sure if it was worth it.

<u>KarmaMart</u>

A thin black streak of tarmac split the darkening desert in two. What vegetation there was out there was hiding in the shadows. Far on either side of the road were massive, impassable slabs of rock. Above, a creeping black void was eating away at what blue shades remained, the remaining few flashes of reds and oranges taking refuge behind the mountains. If ever there was proof of an indifferent God, it was that valley.

On the road a solitary speeding vehicle, its lights incapable of piercing the black soup surrounding it. Paint caked in the dust of a thousand miles, tires sliding down the road like margarine in a pan, the car flit down the road as a descending comet, hurtling toward a bright ball of light some miles further down. Inside sat four strangers, all heading in the same direction, each silently convinced of their own superiority. It had been a quiet drive.

'Will we make it?' said Eunice from behind the driver.

Virgil looked down at the luminous markers behind the wheel. 'We're driving on vapours, but yes. I think so.'

Emergency blinkers dinged to signal they had a different idea. The engine coughed and whimpered, agreeing with the emergency lights. Momentum slowed until the car stopped with a jolt some two miles from the station.

'At least, I thought so,' said Virgil.

'Great,' came a deep voice from the back. 'I knew we should have stopped earlier.' The voice opened a door and stepped out into the darkness.

'Where are you going?'

A slight rock of the car. 'Put it in neutral, we'll push it to the station.'

'There wasn't a station since the last time we filled up, remember?' Samira asked from the passenger seat.

'That was a long time ago, let's just get where we're going and be done with it,' the voice, Clay, called from the behind them, pushing the car forward as he did so, his words strained.

Clay pushed the car alone the whole distance. He was the largest of the group, a former rugby standout whose career ended not with an injury but with a job offer. A flagging sense of chivalry would have prevented him from letting either of the women help, not that they would have considered offering to do so. Virgil, as the driver, was also uninterested in helping. The three of them sat inside in silence, windows wound down, with only the distant crackle of insects, the metallic creaking of an unwilling vehicle pressing forward, and Clay's furtive panting reaching their ears.

They could see it clearer now. Once just a glowing star in the distance, the station beckoned with its blurred, unflickering lights. KarmaMart, letters spelled out with bright red neon bulbs, with a never-closing convenience store hidden behind the glare of the pump stations.

Clay gave the car one final nudge then walked away to catch his breath. The other three couldn't see him for the light. The exited the car and stretched, the creaks and pops of their stiff joints sounded like a popcorn machine.

'Well, then,' said Virgil, still contorting his neck for one last snap. He walked alone into the store.

'I guess I'll pump, then,' said Samari. 'Please don't smoke here.'

'Or what?' said Eunice, smoking.

'They have signs and everything. I guess people like you didn't need to learn to read growing up though.'

'I read fine, thank you.'

'I bet your butler does all the reading. Where is he, anyway? Why even ride with the rest of us?'

'I don't remember.' Eunice flicked the unfinished cigarette into the void. 'There? Happy? Will you shut the fuck up now?'

Samira rolled her eyes as Eunice limped inside. The gas pump stopped, the car full once more. She looked at the tiny digital screen at the price. £170,000,000. A mistake, surely. Definitely. The receipt printed out confirming that, yes, she had just been charged that amount. She snatched the little parchment and stormed into the store.

Inside, Virgil was already arguing with the attendant. He was grasping at a small bag of peanuts with one hand and pointing at the attendant's chest with the other. It was a gesture Samira was acquainted with well, the 'let me talk to your manager' power move of the fabulously wealthy.

'I want to talk to your manager,' said Virgil.

'I am the manager,' said the attendant. His badge said Oengus.

'Well listen here, you cretin, I'm not paying that much for these nuts.'

'No, I know you're not, you're paying that plus a late fee now.'

'The hell I am.'

'This is KarmaMart. You agreed to our terms when you walked through the door. Oh, wait, yes, now there's another late fee.'

'I could buy and sell you, you little pissant, what ma…'

'Then you don't mind paying, then. Hurry, before there's another late fee. Plus interest.'

Virgil sighed and fished through his wallet for his platinum credit card. While he did so, Samira stepped up to the counter.

'Hey,' she said, putting the receipt down, 'This is a mistake, right? There's no way I'm paying this much for gas.'

'Oh, but you already have paid that much for gas, Samira. Already financed and everything.'

'You can't be serious.'

'As I was just trying to explain to your friend here, this is KarmaMart. Everything is based not just on your wealth but your, well, your karma.'

'I run marathons every year, I give money to the homeless, I…'

'Photo op, tax write off, money laundering. Don't pretend you're a good person, Samira; nobody who comes through here is. The fact is you have almost a half billion pounds worth of vacant property you're sitting on. And you want to talk to me about helping the homeless? Please.'

Virgil pushed Samira to one side and slammed his credit card onto the counter. 'Here, you piece of shit, cash me out.'

Oengus chuckled. 'Too late, sir, there were too many late fees so we've had to put a freeze on your assets until the bill is paid in full. Do you have anything else you can pay with?'

'What's your game, buddy? Give me one reason not to jump over this thing and beat the shit out of you.'

'Why would you do that? I'm just trying to make money. How many people do you think your investment firm has ripped off? Killed?'

'Don't take the moral high ground with me. What I do is business.'

'Oh, well, then so is everything I'm doing. That's fair, right? Enjoy the peanuts.'

'This fucking guy.'

Virgil tossed the peanuts onto the floor and walked to the automatic door. Before he could exit, though, a plexiglass cell fell down from the ceiling, encasing him inside. He turned, his face had become a ball of veins and spittle, eyes scrunched and mouth silently screaming at the glass as he banged his fists against his new prison.

Oengus pressed down on a red button and spoke into a microphone. 'You can come out when you've calmed down and paid the cleaning fee,' he said.

'What about me, can I go? I'll be talking to my lawyer,' Samira asked.

'Do whatever you want, but you owe me for air rental now. Half a million for breath. And don't try to leave or I can legally burn you for eternity.'

Samira was a lot more level-headed than Virgil and understood what was happening. She closed her mouth and tried to slow her breathing. If she could just think there was bound to be a way out of it. Just as long as there weren't any distractions.

The door of the ladies' bathroom started banging.

'Hello,' screamed Eunice. 'Hello, I'm trapped inside the bathroom. Can someone let me out?'

Oengus winked at Samira as he walked over to the locked door.

'Is that Eunice?' he asked.

'Yes. Who is this? Let me out please.'

'No can do, babe.'

'Look, I understand you're out there trying to make some kind of point but whatever it is, can you do it with the door open?'

'That's up to you, Eunice.'

'I get it, because I'm rich, right? Well I'm not apologising for the hard work I've put into my brand.'

'Hard work? Your great-grandparents owned slaves. That's where the family wealth came from. Your grandparents, cousins I might add, used their influence to steal land. To steal land. And your parents? Do we even need to discuss them?'

'What's that got to do with me, though? I've done nothing but work hard since I was sixteen.'

'What, modelling for your uncles clothes line?'

'There's the Equality label I started.'

'Oh, yeah, I forgot about that. You can come out now.'

The door jostled. 'Really,' said Eunice.

'Don't pretend that's anything more than a self-serving clothing brand. You've made a billion off of South Asian child labour just so you can pay for a couple of upper middle class suburbanites to go to college. If you were really about equality, no… nothing about you has anything to do about equality, this conversation is over.'

Oengus pressed a small button on the side of the restroom door. Thuds echoed from inside as Eunice tried to force her way out. But it was too late, a barrier began to lower, encasing the ladies' restroom with a thick, impenetrable shell.

'It's like you said,' Oengus shouted, 'Anyone can do what you have done if they dream hard enough. So dream, Eunice. Dream. Anyway, sorry about that, you were saying? Your breathing bill is pretty high, you should probably pay it soon.'

Samira considered it, but she thought back on her career. Even if she paid the breathing fee, there was bound to be some hidden charges waiting for her when she did so. No, unless she wanted to spend her days banging against walls in a desperate attempt to escape, she was going to have to play Karma-Mart at its own game.

'All right, you've got me, I'm a bad person. I'm sorry, OK? It was wrong of me, I've been selfish and greedy and I'm sorry.'

'Oh you're sorry? I'll just change your charges now.'

'Thanks so much.'

Oengus tossed a crumpled receipt at her. 'Except I'm being sarcastic, obviously. What does sorry do? Sorry is a self-serving word for your benefit, not me, not the people you've hurt.'

'I've hurt no one.'

'Get a grip. All those empty houses. You've priced good families out of a livelihood, a future, you're complicit in the deaths of tens of thousands of the homeless, you've held an entire generation of people at ransom. And you've hurt no one? Get fucked.'

Samira began to cry. 'How do I fix this?'

Oengus smiled. 'Finally a good question.'

As he leaned in to explain, the side entrance opened. A small electronic bell chimed overhead. A young couple walked in, woman with child, man beaming. They hovered over the rotating doughnut display while the automatic coffee machine poured out a cappuccino and a decaf tea. The man placed their cups in a tray and held it with one hand and the love of his life with the other. They walked to the counter, deaf to the banging from the restroom, the front entrance, blind to Samira who stood right beside them.

'Is this all?' asked Oengus.

'Oh!' said the pregnant woman, who waddled over to the candy aisle and retrieved a bag of chocolate coated peanuts. She waved them in the air like a triumphant hunter. Her lover looked at her with absolute adoration. They kissed as she placed the bag of chocolate coated peanuts onto the counter.

'Isn't that special,' said Oengus, scanning their good. 'Huh, look at that, this is on the house, guys, have a safe trip.'

'Thank you,' said the man as he picked up their snacks. They floated out the station with their arms interlinked.

'That's how you do it, Samira,' Oengus explained. 'Sorry doesn't change the things you've done or the impact your choices have had on others. It's too late to go back, now, you see. But...'

'But?'

'We're always hiring, Samira. There's a countless number of empty roads just like this one, each with a KarmaMart of its own. The job would do you good, you know. It's a time to reflect. You'll meet a lot of people from a lot of different places. And maybe you'll understand, finally understand, what you didn't most your life.'

Samira looked at Virgil still trying to shoulder way out of the glass, then at the happy couple outside getting back in their car, and finally at the two-for-one special on off-brand cheese balls.

'I was going to be a painter,' she confessed. 'I think I lost my way some-where out there on the road.'

Oengus came out from behind his stall and put a hand on her shoulder.

'You and me both. Come on, I'll get you an application.'

Clay stood engulfed in the darkness outside looking at the glowing blur of the gas station. He had been dreaming of this moment all his life. For years he just thought it an reoccurring nightmare, some latent childhood regret, warped and repressed as the years went by. Inside his reckoning was waiting, a price he could never pay. The things he had done. The things he hadn't done. He had staggered drunkenly onward in life never expecting to pay the bill, but there it was, in all its linoleum and fluorescent glory.

He sat on a rock and looked upward. The sky was vacant, no stars to admire, no final moment of splendour to take with him inside, just a vast darkness that would one day consume him. In the distance a lone coyote yipped as it pursued an anonymous prey. He hadn't heard coyotes since his summer in… Ah, he realised. It was all coming back to him.

'Time to pay up,' he muttered to himself as he pushed himself off his rock and staggered toward the light.

Maybe his life would have played out in a different way if he saw the dreams as a warning, a sign. Maybe. But he didn't, and that was that.

<u>Only the Lonely</u>

Soft red neon broke through the slit in the velvet curtain, cutting the room in half. On one side, an unmade bed consumed by darkness. The other, a desk replete with hotel directory and watermarked sheets of paper. A faint wall of white florescence emanated from the en suite bathroom, incapable of passing through the doorway. The room near-silent but for the hum of outside traffic far below and the infrequent clanking of an antiquated AC unit.

Bruce shuffled between the worlds. It had come to this. He placed two envelopes on the desk, both containing a note and stuffed with unused bills. One addressed TO THE SHIFT MANAGER in the handwriting Bruce reserved for meetings. The other was the fifth envelope of its kind, addressed to the cleaning crew. He wanted that envelope to look as upbeat and familial as an envelope could. Which, he supposed, wasn't much. Short of dotting the Is with hearts and kisses, he was out of ideas.

It was the elusive third letter which was causing him problems. On his walk through the alien city, he thought he had it down pat. A perfectly structured letter he could recite internally as he walked from gallery to public park, down unfamiliar streets, into expensive restaurants. But, as with most writing, by the time he sat down to regurgitate the words onto paper, all he could cough up was bile and glib platitudes.

He sat down and tried to write again. Gripping his mechanical pen, a gift from a dead friend, his hand hovered over a sheet of paper. A sudden pang of guilt. Would the crested watermarks embedded in the pages be considered some tacit endorsement of what he was about to do? Could he be sued post mortem for implicating the hotel? Would it make them look bad? Their service had been exceptional. That reminded him: WRITE A FIVE-STAR REVIEW ON ALL THE APPS BEFOREHAND.

He came up with a solution: the hotel paper would serve only as a first draft. The second draft would have to be written on some borrowed paper from the hotel's world-class business centre. There would be no third draft. A third draft would be sterile and unemotional, a carbon copy, at which point his whole death would be tainted with the humdrum banality of rehearsal, something he'd seen enough of already. Inspiration hit. The first paragraph.

THERE'S A REASON MOST SUICIDES AREN'T PLANNED TOO FAR IN ADVANCE.

THE FURTHER AHEAD, THE MORE IT BECOMES AN OBLIGATION MORE THAN AN ACT OF FREE WILL. SO THAT WOULD BE MY FIRST PIECE OF ADVICE: DON'T CASH OUT YOUR PENSION, SPEND SIX MONTHS TRAVELLING THE WORLD, AND BOOK YOURSELF INTO AN EXPENSIVE (BUT VERY WELL MANAGED AND INTRICATELY DESIGNED) HOTEL ON SOME CARIBBEAN ISLAND. OR DO. I'M NOT IN A POSITION TO TELL YOU WHAT TO DO. I JUST DON'T WANT YOU TO END UP LIKE ME.

He stopped, going back to run multiple lines through the parentheses and everything after the word island. It was a better start than the others. Perhaps as good as the one he couldn't remember when he was outside. No. Bruce didn't want his last night spent critiquing his own suicide note. That was too much, even for a man who spent twenty years converting bereavement into data.

He went back outside.

How fast the heat had escaped the ground. At night, the streets a photo negative of the ones he'd walked through hours earlier. Cold and damp and quiet, with only stray dogs and slow taxis for company. Lurking under porch lights and behind fences, the locals now devoid of welcoming smiles, instead hungry and tired and preparing to start all over again in the morning. Bruce could relate. It gets to a point where there is nothing much left to do but impersonate Sisyphus. Why always Sisyphus? Maybe Prometheus was more apt. After all, he brought light to the… No. Not the time for that.

He walked under darkened skies to the abyss that was once a beach and listened to the waves. In the distance, the melodic beat of steel drums and bongos. Lightning lit up the nothing beyond the horizon. A stray dog had followed him from the cluttered market streets and sat panting somewhere behind him. Bruce closed his eyes and felt the fine tidal mist against his face and the fine white sand between his arthritic fingers. It had been a good visit. But it was time to go.

Back in his room, he hunched once more over the desk.

MY NAME IS BRUCE PICKLING. YOU BARELY KNOW ME. WE MET IN ONE OF A HUNDRED WAYS ALL DIFFERENT YET ALL THE SAME. I WANT YOU TO KNOW WHY I AM DOING THIS BECAUSE I WORRY YOU MIGHT DO THE SAME ONE DAY. PLEASE DON'T BE OFFENDED BY MY PRESUMPTION. JUST… BUT…

Violent erasure of the last sentence, now a jagged black storm cloud on the page.

I HAVE SPENT A THANKLESS LIFE TRYING TO DO THE RIGHT THING. ALWAYS THE RIGHT THING. FOR OTHER PEOPLE. AND BECAUSE OF THIS, I DIDN'T HAVE THE TIME TO BE SELFISH. OH, I WAS ACCUSED OF BEING SELFISH A THOUSAND TIMES, BUT IT WAS NEVER MY INTENT. AND NOW I HAVE NOTHING TO SHOW FOR IT. I AM AT THE TWILIGHT OF MY CAREER, A CAREER I KNOW WILL BE OBSOLETE WITHIN TWO DECADES. I HAVE LEFT BEHIND NO CLOSE FRIENDS, NO CHILDREN, OLD GIRLFRIENDS WHO WILL REMEMBER ME WITH AMBIVALENCE IF ANYTHING AT ALL. IT HAS ALL BEEN FOR NOTHING. AND WHAT WAITS FOR ME IN RETIREMENT? MORE NOTHING. LESS THAN NOTHING. THE SLOW BETRAYAL OF MY OWN BODY. ALREADY MY HANDS ACHE AS I WRITE. IT HURTS WHEN I PISS. I CAN'T WALK UP TWO FLIGHTS OF STAIRS WITHOUT MY KNEES FEELING LIKE THEY WILL IMPLODE. I DON'T MASTURBATE ANY MORE, MUCH LESS GET LAID. DON'T WANT EITHER. THERE WAS A SPARK IN THERE SOMEWHERE WHEN I WAS YOUNG AND IT'S BEEN LOST TO THE AGES. NOW I JUST EXIST. AND ALL TALK OF ENDING IT TO THE FAMILY IS PUT DOWN TO SELFISHNESS. AND MAYBE IT IS. BUT ISN'T IT TIME I DO SOMETHING FOR MYSELF?

The pen lingered over the paper. Bruce made small symbols above certain words. Placed then removed semicolons; he had never understood anything beyond basic punctuation. Underlined words that were too obtuse or overused or archaic. He could never have been a poet. A sudden glimpse at all the lives he was never destined to live: poet, musician, upper management, a professional gambler, private eye, bounty hunter, cage fighter, soap actor, married man. Happy. Sad. A humdrum life of emotional indifference pulled by the gravitational force of minimal effort. But boy could he edit.

Something was missing. A final paragraph. Something to persuade the reader to take more chances. Maybe a drawing. Bruce always wanted someone to look at his doodles but never bothered to show anyone. Not a conversation to easily segue into. "Hey, look at this sketch of a man fighting a giraffe, isn't that great?" his one attempt, an attempt with an ending even a child could guess.

The plan, the last act, was to finish the note and go down to the business centre with its perfect air conditioning and 5G wireless internet speed and ergonomically designed, lumbar-supporting chairs. Go down there in the spacious, expedient elevator, snatch a leaf of plain paper, rewrite the note exactly one time, print out a hundred copies, deposit those copies into the plentiful envelops he'd bought at the airport, address each letter to a younger co-worker or distant relative, a few to newspapers and magazines, return again to the expansive, decadent hotel lobby with the sealed and stamped envelopes, and deposit them into the antique mailbox. Then review the hotel and the tapas place he'd eaten at. A boring, impersonal last act, reminiscent of all the wasted days in cubicles and meetings. He thought perhaps he should do something fun before then. Maybe after. What could be sadder than spending your last night on earth running clerk errands for yourself?

In truth, he didn't even want to end it at a hotel. Yet another concession. It would be cruel to the staff, probably lead to money being deducted from his account before his body went cold, and plus who really wants anyone else to see their corpse? Bruce had wanted to sip piña coladas and walk drunk and happy into the ocean. But then his body may never be found, his letters would make no sense, the hotel would charge him for a few extra nights, and it would take years for what was left of his money to be released from a zero-interest holding account while lawyers and distant relatives sniffed around his property waiting for their chance to pounce.

It was other people. That was the root of everything. Bruce, who had nothing to live for, couldn't imagine living just to exist surrounded by other people. As much as they accused him of only thinking about himself, he lived among a crowd of opportunists, frauds, and liars. It had taken him two months to write his list of one hundred recipients of his suicide note. Two months of extracurricular secretarial research. Fifty some years of pleasing people who couldn't even remember his name half the time. What a joke.

He could feel his pulse tremble through clumped veins, his hands giving the first near-invisible shakes of a sudden change in mood. He would not die angry at hypothetical people. This was his night. His last night. And he refused to spend another second dwelling on faceless, half-remembered people from his past.

So he left the hotel room again, took the stylish, obsidian elevator down to the lobby with the authentic expressionist art on the walls and the plucky, upbeat concierge who was worth a five-star rating all for themselves and walked into the bar.

Dance music pulsed through hidden speakers but no one was dancing. The bar, a frenetic jungle of chrome chairs and strobing lights, was home to five other guests and one large and sleepy bartender. Three of the guests sat slumped over cocktails in private booths watching the swirling light show and bumping their feet out of rhythm with the music. Two sat at the bar close to each other, both in town for a conference, neither attracted to the over but both wanting to feel something. The superficiality of life. Just strangers using each other forever.

Bruce sat at the opposite side of the bar and watched the temporary couple, the secret dancers lingering beside an empty dance floor. The bartender arrived with a vacant face and couldn't find the effort to fully shrug let alone speak. Bruce was confronted with the sudden knowledge he was choosing his last ever drink. What to have? Scotch? Expensive, unpronounceable scotch from some tiny distillery? A cocktail that would spike his blood sugar and heart rate at just the wrong time? Vodka something? Straight rum? He gestured vaguely at the menagerie of half-finished bottles. The bartender grabbed something Bruce couldn't quite make out. He nodded anyway. Leave it up to the universe. It's what you've been doing your whole life. Little knowing the universe doesn't care because the universe has no brain, no heart, no feelings. A wistful recollection of old friends carried on by waves of creativity and ambition, entrusting in some cosmic helping hand, only to wind up dead or penniless or lost to immeasurable indifference. At least Bruce's meandering was tied to the reality that nothing truly mattered. The one thing to get him through life unmolested.

And there was the rub. Taking no chances, in the end, was just as unfulfilling and stultifying as any of the other paths people had chosen. No matter. It would be over soon. One act of free will then it's Cinco dos adios from old Bruce.

He sipped his drink. Peach schnapps.

From out of a booth a stranger made tentative steps to the dancefloor, spun around, and returned to their imaginary world where they had the nerve to dance uninhibited. The couple at the bar, with dead fish eyes, and the limp, detached mannerisms of a gynaecologist, began to kiss. A slobbering, drunk, passionless kiss that promised a night of unfulfilling rutting and a morning of contemplation and regret.

Bruce returned to his room.

I WROTE THIS TO YOU AND NINETY-NINE OTHERS. I DO NOT REGRET MY LIFE BUT RATHER FEEL NOTHING ONE WAY OR THE OTHER. AND THAT'S ENOUGH FOR ME. I'M OUT. THIS WAS SENT TO YOU BECAUSE I THINK YOU STILL HAVE—I WOULDN'T SAY HOPE EXACTLY—BUT LIFE IS MEANINGLESS AND QUICK AND STUPID, AND IT'S EASY TO GET LOST IN THE MINUTIAE OF THE DAY TO DAY AND WAKE UP AT FIFTY-SIX WITH NOTHING BUT A PENSION FUND, A MORTGAGE, A PACK OF VAGUE IDEAS PASSING AS MEMORIES, AND A BODY THAT'S FAILING. AND BESIDES ALL OF WHICH, EVEN IF I WERE IN PERFECT WORKING ORDER WITH A WIFE AND CHILDREN AND THREE HOUSES AND A JOB TITLE WITH MEANING BEHIND IT, WHAT'S TO LOOK FORWARD TO? EVEN THEN. A WIFE WHO WOULD DIE AND CHILDREN WHO WOULD MOVE AWAY OR WATCH YOU DIE OR BOTH. THE SUDDEN AND HUMBLING REALISATION YOU ARE COMPLETELY MEANINGLESS IN ANY SENSE OF THE WORD AND THE WORLD OUTSIDE IS BURNING. WHO WANTS TO SIT THROUGH ARMAGEDDON? FOOD SHORTAGES? WARS? THE SORT OF OBVIOUS AND HORRIFYING TERRORS OF MODERN LIVING YOU CAN BOTH ACKNOWLEDGE AND DO NOTHING ABOUT? I DON'T WANT ANYTHING TO DO WITH THOSE THINGS.

I SAID MEANINGLESS A FEW TIMES. BUT THAT'S LIBERATING IN ITS OWN WAY. BECAUSE IF LIFE MEANS NOTHING, YOU GET TO DECIDE YOUR OWN DEFINITIONS. UNLIKE ME. SO MAYBE TAKE THAT FROM THIS NOTE IF YOU TAKE ANYTHING AT ALL. YOU CAN DEFINE HOW YOU LIVE BECAUSE IT'S ALL JUST PISS IN THE RAIN ANYWAY. THANKS FOR READING THIS FAR.

PLEASE FIND ENCLOSED A SMALL AMOUNT OF MONEY AS AN APOLOGY FOR MAKING YOU READ THIS NOTE WITHOUT FIRST ACQUIRING YOUR CONSENT. I'M SURE UNWITTINGLY READING A SUICIDE NOTE IS INVASIVE IN WAYS I AM NOT EVEN CONSIDERING RIGHT NOW.

SINCERELY Y…
   IN GOOD F…
   NOMINALLY…
   WARM REGARDS
   BRUCE PICKLING.

He needled through his writing with medical precision, fishing out adverbs and adjectives and searching for all the times he'd used the words "that," "just," and "maybe." Words he would never allow himself to use in a final draft. Too clunky. Too overused. Completely against the message of The Elements of Style. Once finished, his note was littered with a labyrinth of lines and arrows and squiggly lines and missives to himself. To anyone else, it would appear to be the ravings of an engineer.

He went down to the business centre with the business edition of Office on every computer and the complimentary, branded ink gel pens. He sat in a corner and rewrote his note with the appropriate edits, looked over it once, twice, reminded himself of his promise to make no more edits, and walked over to the photocopier, scanning his room key on the side to put the printing costs on the bill he would pay as a ghost, and printing out one hundred and thirteen copies. The extra thirteen were in case of some administrative error while stuffing the envelopes.

His return to the room was more melancholy than he expected. His mind was ready but it was as if his body sensed the impending end of its being and mourned its death through plodding footsteps, clenched fists, twitching eyelids.

He placed the papers on the desk and turned out the lights to his room. The television kicked on automatically. A hotel menu page with repetitive adverts for activities not currently in season. Almost enough to affect the review. Almost

As he fished out the envelopes from his suitcase, something his him. A bolt of inspiration. He retrieved his pen from his pocket and rushed to the copied sheets of paper.

I HAD MANY CHOICES IN LIFE, BUT THIS WAS THE FIRST ONE I CHOSE.

BECAUSE CHOICES ARE MADE FOR YOU WHETHER YOU HAVE INPUT OR NOT.

SOMETIMES DOING NOTHING IS A CHOICE OF ITS OWN.

Close enough. He wrote the addition to each of the hundred sheets of paper, some with different word choices, others with scratches and inkblots. Oddly personalised suicide notes. A nice touch. Bruce himself would appreciate such a decision. Especially if people got together and compared notes. Which he supposed was a possibility.

Well. He sighed. All over but the stuffing. He finished his administrative tasks with the speed of an employee too aware of how close they are to the end of their shift. He stamped and licked and hauled them down to the lobby with the grand piano and the receptionist with the welcoming aura and great customer service skills and dropped the letters one by one into the antique English mailbox.

Then he pulled the rope he'd bought from the yellow plastic shopping bag. It had taken him a whole day to find the right rope. Pushed plans back a day.

He entered the bathroom, all white light and marble and mirrors. Heaven, but for his reflection. It took three attempts to get the noose right, but there it was. Perfect. And.

His phone rang. He walked to it despite himself. A cousin was calling. His hand hovered over the phone, eyes looking back at the bathroom. It was not in his nature to ignore a phone call. "Hello?"

Sobs. "Oh, it's awful, Bruce."

"What is it?"

"It's Aunt Madeline. She's gone missing."

The soft red neon cut through the velvet curtain. A faint line of pink light severed the room in two. On one side, Bruce on his bed, phone in his hand, the inescapable expectations of others crying through the telephone. The other, a desk replete with notes to hotel staff and unused copies of a suicide letter. A faint wall of white florescence emanated from the en suite bathroom, incapable of passing through the doorway. The room near-silent but for the hum of outside traffic far below and the infrequent clanking of an antiquated AC unit.

Let Me Show You how it Feels

1.

If you ever want to surprise yourself - or confirm what you already know, depending on your POV - ask some of your friends and family about their worst dating experiences. Invariably, your straight male friends will, if they're being honest, talk about rejection, maybe some manipulation, something ego-killing and embarrassing, but relatively harmless, albeit potentially psyche destroying. Maybe a woman led him to believe they'd have sex and then, the horror, didn't want to have sex, the cockteasing bitch. The women in your life, however, will more than likely talk about being stalked, threatened, cajoled, assaulted to varying degrees. A date went poorly, say, but since he paid for dinner, she let him walk her home, only then, once they got there he forced his way in and she was confronted with the very real possibility of getting murdered, so she let him have sex with her as some sort of hideous compromise. The difference in the stories will be fairly evident, and while it would be unlikely all women's tales went to those extremes, they will, by and large, carry a different weight to them than most of the men you talk to. There will be some exceptions, obviously.

And this is only considering a fairly heteronormative perspective. Ask your gay, your bi, your trans friends (and if you don't have any, get some) and they will likely have some fairly harrowing tales of their own. Remember, though: these are people who weren't brutally murdered during their worst dating experience, so your sampling will never reveal the whole spectrum of experiences.

It's not a particularly fun game, but it's one you should all play at least once.

2

The device had initially been designed for crime scene units and the police to access the feelings of victims of various crimes. They would strap someone into the machine and that person would experience what the recently deceased felt, for example. It was the hope of these investigators to glean a slightly more clear insight into the acts of violence they were investigating. Unfortunately, the results were largely useless in most situations, too limited in scope to reveal anything that old fashioned police work couldn't accomplish. Plus too, experiencing a brutal murder wasn't exactly what most people wanted to sit through, so it was often difficult to find volunteers willing to strap in to the device. Those who were willing were often perhaps a little too eager, which yielded more problems than quantifiable results. In the end, the device was deemed both scientifically miraculous and completely useless.

It was only when the rights to the machine were bought by a pornography conglomerate that its true potential truly presented itself. For a reasonable price, people from all over the world could, from the safety of their own computer chair, strap in and fully experience whatever flavour of sex they did so wish. If they wanted to pretend to fuck the babysitter, and many of them did, now they could experience the whole act; feel the skin, the dampness, the warmth of her breath, her nubile fingers digging into *their* back. Any sex act you could imagine, you could experience from a perspective of your choice, for a nominal fee, and as far as your brain was concerned, you were actually there. Orgasms without digital manipulation. Very real sensations etched into brains for years to come, as memorable as any actual life event.

Productivity in the workplace started to increase after stagnating for decades. Unhappy marriages were rendered surprisingly content. The confidence in disillusioned young men all over the world sky-rocketed, with a not-incidental drop in terrorism, paramilitary recruitment, and sales in testosterone booster placebos. The porn conglomerate became the wealthiest entity on the planet, with several billionaires seeing their own stock prices plummet as people overnight lost interest in whatever it was their companies were selling. No singular event had changed the world as quickly - unless you count global extinction events, which for the purpose of this story, you shouldn't.

Unfortunately, as with so many cases where sex and money are involved, it wasn't long before people, men mostly, found a way to ruin it. Jaded former boyfriends of Oscar winning actresses began selling their hazy recollections of drunken fumbles with the starlets. High school lovers of promising political candidates, selling their fetid half-memories to tabloid newspapers for six figures, all to discredit someone who wanted to deliver something evil to their people, like affordable healthcare or clean water (their opponents, largely, grey old men whose former lovers had died many decades earlier). There were karmic acts of justice, self-proclaimed Lotharios were outed as lame lays, and a plethora of homophobic figureheads were presented with the incontrovertible evidence of their own sodomy, beamed directly into the confused minds of their own constituents. For the most part, though, predatory people had found a new stream of revenue for their disturbing behaviour, and the general public were more than happy to sneakily buy up whatever experiences they could think of.

"Taking child-actress virginity @_@ REAL SEX WITH CHILD STAR @_@," "Fucking Prime Minister's Arsehole EX BOYFRIEND LETS YOU RELIVE IT ALL," and "REAL AUTHENTIC SERIAL KILLER MEMORIES" were the sorts of titles that garnered the most attention. Anything truly revelatory or, indeed, erotic, quickly became lost under a sea of smut and voyeurism, the likes of which were hitherto unimaginable. While the device's early days had ushered in a new era of happiness and fulfilment, they had quickly been replaced by a darkness, a meanness that seemed poised to damn entire continents. And why wouldn't they? Any dark craving was suddenly not only available, but liveable.

3.

Vivien Gaynor sat poolside at the Palais Impuissant, feeling the LA sun find its way through her third sunscreen application of the day. She owed a lot to her fine porcelain skin - her entire career, really - so taking care of it was the least she could do. Sure, there were times when her fanbase creeped her out, her 49.3 million followers mostly innocuous, but all seeming to want more from her than she was willing to give. You're nowhere without your fans, her publicist would tell her, even if half of them think you're the thirteen year old character you played fifteen years ago, and the other half…

"You know you've got your own pool, right?" her agent, Patrick, said.

"But it's so boring sitting alone."

Patrick looked around. "But you're sitting alone now?"

"Yes, but here I get to watch."

Patrick nodded. "Speaking of, I've got something… a bit of a weird offer for you."

Vivien was watching the children of a producer repeatedly run and jump into the pool. As the only children staying at Palais Impuissant, they were something of an annoyance to the rest of the guests. The producer would apologetically look at the smattering of swimmers he deemed important enough to look at. She didn't want to have the conversation she knew she was about to have.

"I don't want to have this conversation," Vivien said.

"Fifty million dollars, and it's maybe half an hours work. If you can call it work."

"I call it exploitative, invasive, and immoral."

"I appreciate your opinion, Vivien, really I do. But just think of the good you can do with that money. And besides, we both know you've already had sex with Blake Cagney, so it wouldn't exactly be uncharted ter…"

"Blake and I enjoyed a private, personal declaration of mutual admiration, once, five years ago. It's a cherished memory, and I want it to stay that way."

"Look, I understand this is a difficult topic to even broach, Vivien, but it's only a matter of time before someone else comes forward with footage of you having sex."

Vivien sighed. The children had recruited a reluctant ninety year old actor into a game of keep away. "Patrick, I appreciate the work you've done for me, but you're about three seconds away from needing a new client list. This is absolutely disgusting on so many levels. Please drop it. If some limpid jagoff failed actor wants to sell their whiskey dicked recollections of a regrettable night in El Estandar to the media, then so be it. Anyone I've shared a genuine experience with, I trust explicitly."

Vivien felt something tugging at the edges of her subconscious.

"I understand. Sorry I brought it up, Viv. Just fifty million is a lot of money."

"I could retire right now, Patrick. Right now. Some things just aren't even worth thinking about, no matter what sort of price tag is attached. Now, let's just drop the whole thing. Any other offers for me?"

Patrick let out a laugh of relief. "How'd you feel about playing Artemis in a cyberpunk retelling of the Iliad?"

"Somehow, that's a worse offer."

4.

Vivien couldn't sleep that night. Barring a handful of thirty second mistake, her sexual encounters had been respectful, with partners she trusted. Even the evening with Blake Cagney had been enjoyable if not a little sterile. All encounters but one, at least. But Vivien tried her best to act as if it had never happened. Occasionally, she'd look up the old man's obituary to remind herself that he was dead. Even as she tried to force herself into unconsciousness in her hotel bedroom, plaudits and glowing remembrances of a long dead man were being written. She sat up and looked through the most recent essays on the deceased's glorious career. Hard to believe it was the same man who. But, as she'd frequently been told, a man with such passion for art, he just lets that passion get the better of him some time.

Vivien got out of bed. When memories of the dead man came back, the bed was the last place she wanted to be. She had stopped believing in ghosts before she reached puberty, but his was a spectre that would never leave.

The offer of fifty million dollars was emblematic of a larger problem. This sense of male entitlement permeating through everything, destroying everything. By her estimation at least. The initial success had allowed the disadvantaged, the socially anaemic, the isolated and the scared to enjoy experiences they'd otherwise never be able to fully enjoy. But the fifty million offer was signs of things to come, perhaps the way things had already been for some time. They, whoever they were, had found just another way to have non-consensual sex. And, sure, they weren't physically with people, just experiencing a sequence of brainwaves that manipulated their nervous system, but. But. But. There were implications. Things these people need to understand. It was wrong on levels that were hard to put into words for Vivien at 3AM.

Put into words.

She reached for her phone and dialled.

"Vivien? Look, I'm sorry about today, I regret even bringing it up."

"No, it's OK. I accept, on two conditions: I want one hundred million and total creative control."

"Y… Wow. That's quite the change of heart. I'm sure they'll agree to your terms. What about Blake, though?"

"Don't worry about him. Night Patrick."

5.

It was the most publicised event of the year. Vivien Gaynor and Blake Cagney were going to have sex, live, while hooked up to the device. Over a billion people had pre-ordered the PPV, with another five hundred million expected to log in on the day. The revenue was monumental. Vivian and Blake had shrewdly negotiated fifty percent between them, but even so the porn conglomerate had cemented itself as the most successful entity to ever exist. Even while political leaders were exposed, arrested, assassinated, even while royal families were declared insolvent, and entire countries sank into the ocean, the collective media couldn't stop talking about the fact that two very successful and critically acclaimed actors were going to let so many people experience their lovemaking.

All around the world, men were hosting sweaty watch parties, with strategic partitions between each guest. Normally, when using the device, the entire experience would be pumped into your psyche with a jolt, a sudden dump of information, a five second information exchange. But to experience the whole thing live? With the girl who played the wizard in that one film? And the superhero guy with the abs? It was an experience that was hard to refuse. For some at least.

There were protests. And, as Vivien and Blake walked into their studio to record their session, they were confronted by hundreds of angry women and their allies. Irate, betrayed, concerned. Scared. Vivien was glad. It meant they weren't going to be tuned in for the show. Strangely, many of the religious leaders and talking heads who had publicly lambasted the performance only hours earlier had decided against attending the protests, instead locking themselves in their offices and turning off their phones. Surely, they were so upset with the state of the world that they had sequestered themselves so they might not see what was about occur.

Sitting at the edge of the bed in an otherwise empty studio, a moustachioed comedian looked at the stationary camera. His three-piece suit and general demeanour were about as far removed from a live sex show as conceivably possible, but nevertheless, there he was. Grinning at the camera.

"Well, I never thought my largest audience would be introducing two other people having sex," said the comedian. "But here we are. You remember them both from their careers, and you probably don't know who I am, but we're all here to watch Vivien Gaynor and Blake Cagney have sex. I wanted to use the F-word there, but apparently that's not allowed even though we're about to… well. Anyway. Without further ado, welcome to the show."

Vivien was first into the studio. The comedian brushed past her quickly, unable to make eye contact with her. She sat on the soft, silk sheets of the giant bed and stared, expressionless, at the camera. Many of her billion plus viewers felt a knot of anticipation tighten deep inside them. Some struggled with the urge to masturbate - it seemed to defeat the purpose, but they were so eager to see her there. Feel her there.

Blake joined her, awkwardly, clumsily, sitting at the edge of the bed. It was about to happen. They waited for a moment, as the latecomers hooked themselves up to their portable devices. Like when the cinema was still a fun place to visit, there would be no late admittance, and once hooked in, you were hooked in for the rest of the show.

"Hi everyone," said Vivien, slowly taking off her shirt. "I really hope you enjoy what you're about to see."

And then.

6.

At first, the viewers slowly eased into the sensations they were experiencing. Vivien topless, nervous, short of breath. Blake's hands cupping her breasts, his penis slowly slithering to attention, his lips gently nestling into her marble jawline. Blake, too, removed his shirt, and they fell into to bed. The viewers in their cubicles eased themselves into the experience, incapable of backing out even if they wanted to, ready for what they hoped would be a life changing experience.

And then a hard cut to a memory dump of Vivien's rape. Unwanted hands grasping at her hair, her frustration suddenly tangible, the sense of betrayal in her own body as alien objects found their way inside her. Desperate attempts to escape, to forget, to dull her own senses. Helplessness. Some futile childish hope that someone would rescue her. Memories of the aftermath. The shame. "Why would you want to ruin someone's career like that after all he did for you?" "Oh, like you didn't want to, you evil little bitch." The shame. The permanence of shame. The loss of friends. The consolatory job offers, the accusations of fucking her way to the top. Always the shame. The pain. The sleepless nights. The nightmares. The inability to trust good men. "Well it was worth it if it got you this deal," and the contempt Vivien felt for hearing those words from her own mother. All suddenly too real, and too recent, beamed directly into almost two billion brains. If they thought the dusky memories of drunken one night stands with pre-fame starlets were surprisingly serviceable memory dumps, they hadn't banked on how all encompassing memories of assault and violation could be.

Blake, too, had memories. Early efforts to make it as an actor. Clammy older people objectifying him. A sexuality fully explored without permission, ruined before a true maiden voyage. The impossibility of living as a man who would never truly know what his sexuality was, because the ability to figure it out had been robbed of him by horny producers before he could legally drink. But drink he did. The slow slog of reclaiming his own soul, trying to make a mist of self-hatred and medication clear away long enough The constant regret and frustration. If he'd been a real man. A real man. Self-accusatory nights besides the noose, the razor, the needle, the gun. The abject horror of being treated like consumable goods and knowing that you'll never be able to fully talk about it, because even if people believed you, a significant portion would downplay it in a million tiny but hurtful ways. You were a punchline at best and a forgotten statistic at worst.

And so, too, were the memories of the hundred or so victims Vivien had gathered in the adjoining studio. All hooked up to the device, ready to dump their experiences into the minds of the spectators back home. All 1,985,636,355 of them.

7.

Vivien sat at her own pool that night, not entirely sure if what she had done was the right thing. Her ride back to the hotel had been a quiet one. She had turned off her phone hours ago, and didn't much care to talk to anyone. Outside, people walked around much as they ever had, and it was impossible for her in that moment to figure out who had watched the stream. Statistically at least a few of those she saw had chosen to do so. They couldn't have all sequestered themselves in their rooms.   Maybe she'd accomplished nothing?

She could hear only the sounds of traffic and clanking glasses beyond her fenced in private pool. The sky was poisoned by orange light, dark but starless, and for the first time in years, Vivien felt at peace. She would sleep soundly without assistance and, in the morning, see what sort of world she'd created.

8.

If you ever want to surprise yourself - or confirm what you already know, depending on your POV - ask some of your friends and family about the worst sexual experience they've ever had. Invariably, most people will, if they're being honest, talk about a failure to perform, an embarrassing, scatological incident, maybe some sort of strain or rupture that was, in the moment traumatic ego-killing, but largely and ultimately innocuous. Some, however, more than you care to realise, will share a story that will eat away at your soul if you care enough to listen.

<u>The MV, Or;</u>
<u>Outline for Act One of a Pilot</u>

'Look around. No guards. Unless… a googly eavesdropper?' Irma Said. 'Anyway. Very interesting report. Umbrella, sir?'

As the patient dug through the pockets of her voluminous gown, Horatio Kamau couldn't help but gawk at her. Had she not noticed the imposing warden standing over her? Could she not see the group of faces staring through the pane behind him? He thought back to her most recent employee photo, taken mere months earlier. The Irma of the photograph had an unaging face and starlit eyes, an upbeat health enthusiast. That woman, her bright self, was nowhere within the ghoul facing him, it was more akin to attending an open casket funeral.

'News!' she exclaimed while extracting a small plastic figurine from her front pocket. A bundle of scrawled notes spiller out of her clenched fist and fell to the floor. Horatio opened his hand and received a miniature brown deer. She presented it with a grin on her face like she had solved his many problems. All he could muster was the limp smile of the unsatisfied.

'Great! Thank you! I appreciate this!' Horatio was unsure if his polite facade was worth the effort - she wouldn't remember in the morning. 'But the matter at hand: Where is Abraham?'

'Unknown.' Good, a direct answer. A first.

'Any idea where he is going? What his plans are? It's important we find him? People are getting hurt.'

'Goes to bible tech. Hides germs in livers.'

Emitting a low sigh, Horatio nodded at the attending guard and left Irma to her jumbled thoughts. He had wasted another morning on dead-ends and could feel the time ebb away. At least he could give the toy to someone. Small favours. He followed the guard through the labyrinth of sterile corridors. Bone white, dingy, cavernous hallways from centuries ago. Disembodied murmurs and wordless chants broke through the white noise of echoing footsteps and followed him outside. The place was all but haunted.

'Is she going to be OK?' he asked the doctor smoking near the exit. They had talked when Horatio entered the ward, but he had excused himself at the first opportunity.

'She's losing a fight to an invisible monster, I expect she'll be dead soon.'

'And you're no closer to the cause?'

'Very astute, but Isn't that your job, Mister Kamau? We're seeing new symptoms every day, but no. No explanation.'

'Is it possible this is just extreme depression? She saw her colleagues kill themselves.'

'Researchers, yeah? And no, depression doesn't lead to this kind of deterioration.'

Unannounced thunder claps rumbled somewhere behind the building. The sky was darkening. Flicking their cigarettes onto the unkempt lawn, the doctor and his smoking buddies jogged back inside. Horatio walked down the path to the security checkpoint. He turned for one last glimpse at the psych ward, hoping a hidden clue would reveal itself.'

'Schmuck,' he spat.

'Show you something?' a voice from a doorway.

Horatio was almost at the station. He spun around, a bedraggled man in a grey uniform was sitting hunched against the wall. 'Huh?'

'I have something to show you.'

As Horatio stepped nearer, the pungent aroma of mulled urine and unwashed body parts dispelled his initial curiosity. On closer inspection, the man had been festering in his own filth for days.

'Thanks, but I have a train to catch,' Horatio called out as he ran.

Crowds of indignant commuters packed the station, some of whom were quick to declare they had been there for some time. Horatio looked over at the information booth and found it closed. Up above, the LED board was still relaying yesterday's messages.

'Metro is out,' said a bemused spectator. 'There were two jumpers and then half the staff quit. Which is fair enough, except they waited three hours to announce it.'

'*... we have suspended your scheduled rail services because of...*' a speaker announced. Groans from the masses who would remain where they stood to fight for a seat whenever a train arrived. Horatio thought of the approaching storm, imagined the melee of impatient commuters, and ran back to work.

The ground floor offices were dark when he entered. Phones rang unanswered in the back cubicles. The automatic, overhead lights which switched on as Horatio passed through the foyer consumed a blue hue of abandoned monitors. The storm outside rattled the windows. A low, metallic hum of a hundred hibernating machines echoed in his ears.

As he made his way to his locker, a figure appeared from the balcony above. His supervisor, Bill, a man who would delegate his own bathroom breaks if the technology was available, was looking over the railing from the next floor.

'Kamau, thank god, get up here. I have something to show you.'

His shoes hit each step with a squelch as he trudged up the stairs. Horatio discovered most of his colleagues had gathered in the briefing room. They were staring at a chunk of text scribbled on the whiteboard.

'What's this?' Horatio panted.

His manager pointed at the board. 'We found this encrypted in Larunda's suicide note. What do you make of this?'

Larunda Underquay, Irma Induco, Abraham
Aygros, Sachairi Redeo. Now Gone.
All units gone. Eliminated. Virus. Save

Someone had circled the word virus multiple times by varying shades of red marker. Green ink trailed off from each of the names leading to concise factoid. They had arranged each doctor's fate (missing, suicide, institutionalised) in patterns on a separate board. It was all -

'We think at least one of them figured out that Abraham had some dangerous ideas. They wanted to send a warning, and we let him get away,' Bill scanned the room for accusatory glances. 'This may sound morbid, but the incidents yesterday will deflect some eyes off us, but we've overlooked something. Abraham is out there and we don't know what he's planning.'

Bill clapped his hands and the rest of the team got to their feet. Forced to shout over them like a teacher after the bell, he said 'Double check everything, people. There must be information we haven't seen. I want someone calling toxicology every ten minutes until they get back with their results. Horatio, a minute.'

The two of them stood in silence until the other workers returned to their cubicles downstairs. The building came to life within moments. 'How is Irma? Did she have anything?'

'Just this,' Horatio tossed the plastic deer to him. 'She's as good as gone, though.'

'Shame. That complicates things. I need you to take a car to the CRLM facility; I'm betting someone missed vital information the first time.'

Horatio nodded and made to leave, but his supervisor grabbed him by the elbow. 'And listen: we're this close to this going public. Too much has leaked already, and I don't think it's a coincidence three people didn't up today. Share nothing with anyone but me until we've got something concrete.'

'Wow, so they think he's made a pathogen now,' said Abigail Astermoy of the Evening Press. 'Shit, it seems like only yesterday this was just a death pact gone wrong. What next, nuclear weapons?'

'We don't know it's a virus for sure. The person who wrote it immolated themselves half an hour later.'

They had met at a gas station ten minutes away from the forest. Abigail drove her car along the private road to the laboratory. Thick oak surrounded them, the location was a guarded secret. It had taken CRLM's groundskeeper three days to check on the property, to find the bodies, Irma languishing in the middle of a ransacked personal library.

Abigail pressed on the brakes as the security gate came into view. Horatio stepped out the car and made his way to the booth, excuses forming in his mind. As he approached the window, he became concerned that no guard was rising out of the shadows to greet him. Through the booth's open door, he saw that no one was inside. A half dozen coffee mugs littered the work desk, and a paperback sat face down on the stool. A fine layer of silt had accumulated on the surfaces. He waved at Abigail, gesturing their safety.

They parked in the gravel lot away from the main building. Horatio thought of upscale rehab clinics and wellness retreats, not that he had spent too much time at either. He half-expected a porter in an all-white uniform to come running around the corner, chasing a patient. Abigail was mumbling adjectives to herself, an article already forming in her head.

'Did you read my piece on the trading scandal?' she asked.

'I don't pay attention to politics, Abie, we've been through this. It's a bunch of corrupt people lost in semantics. We've got more problems. Bigger ones.'

'That's a lot of words to say you didn't read it.'

'Here's the thing, though, I don't have to even look at it. I can pretend I did, like everyone else.'

'I wish I'd have known you were such a plebe when we first met.'

'Yeah, well,' he paused as they reached the building's entrance. 'The common cold was the only thing they detected when they swabbed inside.'

'Please, I'm more worried about the unavenged ghosts of the dead than I am catching a made up virus. I'm almost certain this is a smoke screen, trust me. But you go first.'

Horatio peeled the cautionary tape from the door and pushed it open. The lobby of the laboratory was barren. Two semi-circular staircases lead up to a second floor, the round room ahead gave way to a row of glass rooms. A rickety metal elevator hid under the left staircase leading down where the guards found the bodies.

Abigail gestured at the lift. 'Where does that go?'

'Hell,' said Horatio. 'That's where it all happened.'

She smiled and approached the steel gate. 'Shall we?'

The elevator took them down to another annular room, with four doors leading to each of the doctors' private suites. Whoever decorated had done so in the seventies; the design of the green carpet, the faux-wood walls, the orange velour lamps were a testament to a bygone age. A dark patch of floor was hard to ignore. It was on that spot they found Doctor Redeo, with an assortment of scalpels. The cleaning crew couldn't scrub the stain away.

'Which door first?' asked Horatio.

'Room number two, please.'

'Oh, unlucky,' Horatio walked into the apartment revealing its empty insides. 'This was Abraham's place. They've already packed everything here up and shipped it back to the office.'

Abigail glanced at the ducts, the edges of the floor. 'I might find something stashed away. No way does a guy like Abraham not have hidden compartments.'

'Good luck, we checked everywhere.'

While Abigail rattled, tapped, slapped, and knocked every surface she could in Abraham's suite, Horatio searched through the other three. They had already taken their personal computers and books, but most of their more harmless mementoes remained. Sachairi's private collection of sketches still clung to his walls. Irma's room had been less lucky - as most of her possessions were books, all that remained were the shelves and pencils.

'Shame, I had almost convinced myself I would find something,' said Abigail as she entered the chamber. 'Whose place was this?'

'Irma's; they took her books already, so unless you want to tap the walls again, we've got one room left.'

Larunda's suite was virtually untouched. There were distinct gaps in the dust from where her electronics had been, but a shelf full of trinkets remained on the wall. Origami cranes of varying sizes and the variety of chintz found in fairgrounds stood in order of size. At the end of the row was a plastic deer. Horatio picked it up and held it close to his face.

'Irma had one of these.'

'Oh these,' said Abigail, 'Give it here.'

She put her fingers on the deer's nose and belly and squeezed. A concealed USB stick popped out from a tiny rubber slit where its anus should be. 'See,' Abigail smile, 'I told you I would find something.'

'You were talking about secret compartments and you know it.'

'Early days yet, Kamau. Shall we?'

They made their way to the observation level. Horatio felt with a sudden pang of obligation and called his supervisor. As he did so, Abigail took large strides across the open floor, sussing the area out.

'Found anything?'

'We, I guess so. There is a drive inside the deer I showed you. Push on its tummy.'

'It's wh… ah! Ha, yeah, that sure is a neat trick. And a noted scientist gave this to you?'

'A borderline catatonic noted scientist, yes.'

'Well don't let me stop you.'

As Horatio hung up, Abigail ran out of the building. He paused, awaiting her to return, and within minutes she appeared skipping up the stairs.

'This floor has more wall outside than it does in this room.'

He looked around the room, a bare attic space that had once served as CRLM's office. The ceiling hung low, the windows were tiny, it was a far from an ideal working environment. If they had extra space, they would have used it.

'Most buildings do that because of, you know, insulation.'

'No building needs nine feet of insulation. Come on, help me find the switch.'

'Is your house made up of hidden switches?'

'If you spent more time there, you'd see. Now shut up and look.'

Horatio ran his hands across the walls while Abigail crouched under heel rapping her knuckles against the lower sections. He had to creep so as not to stand on her toes. They searched two sides this way before Abigail caught a glimpse of something. 'Ah-ha!' she said and rammed her index finger under a protruding knot of wood.

Horatio was ready to shake his head when a large panel on the far wall creaked open revealing a second office. Abigail leapt to her feet and ran inside.

The hidden room had been untouched by the cleaning crew. A single computer lay on a desk in the corner and a network of tiny monitors hung from the ceiling, showing live recordings of the vacant glass rooms below. Smeared equations covered a whiteboard. An empty folder entitled MV sat on the table.

'Were any MVs working here?' Abigail asked.

'No. Listen, before you go screwing around, remember that nobody back at the office knows about this.'

Too late, Abigail jammed her thumb into the console booting up the computer. 'Oops, I slipped, honest.'

The computer's monitor lit up to show a titan eating what remained of a human body. A single folder labelled 'Subjects 1-99' hovered above the creatures head. Abigail clicked it without thinking. Horatio was rethinking her involvement, not that his opinion mattered any more.

Each file on screen was a time lapse video of one of the ground floor cubicles. They showed various test Subjects staring at small monitors, sheets of paper, books. Then nothing. Most would sit in their cubicle for an extended period before falling asleep or released. It wasn't until Subject 53 that things became more animated. As before, they looked at a monitor, and then sat still, but somewhere around the three-hour marker, they snapped. Subject 53 began to kick at the door and ram their forehead against the wall before the video ended without warning. Other Subjects exhibited similar symptoms, some projecting their sudden rage outward at the room, others started to self-harm.

'I can't watch any more of these,' said Abigail, after seeing what happened to Subject 67.

'We have enough. Let's call it in, I'll get you home.'

'Wait,' she said, sliding the deer's USB stick into a vacant drive. A new folder appeared on the screen. 'Let me show you something,' was the title.

'Should we do this?' Horatio replied, a bubbling sense of dread rising in his stomach.

'Sure,' said Abigail. She clicked the folder to show a single file. MV was its name, and it read like this:

Shake hemlock's arm, reinvent extinction.
Takes hands in self-annihilation.
Necessary destruction demands irradiation. End.

Abigail rolled her eyes. 'One of the worst haiku I've ever seen. Whose thirteen-year-old son wrote this?'

'Maybe it's a clue or something. There's a reason Larunda hid it.'

'Oh yeah, wasn't she supposed to be a professor in language? And I can't even find an agent, typical. I'm taking a photo of this, hope you don't mind.'

'Whatever, not like I have a choice. Just make sure you cover…'

'Our tracks, I remember. I'll say it came from someone who claims to be Abraham. That'll give the story more zest, anyway. I better get to work if I want this on tomorrow's front page. Shall we?'

They left the CRLM facility at a speed neither thought possible and parted ways at the gas station. Horatio made his way back to the office in silence. The radio had breaking news on a fresh round of shootings and an apparent suicide pact at a nearby factory. He drove the rest of the way back listening to old music.

The station was once again dark when he returned. Chairs lay strewn on the floor, and someone had left several cubicles in a state of disarray. Horatio glanced around expecting to discover something horrible; all he could see was a mess. They'd taken off in a hurry. Walking up the stairs to the supervisor's office he knocked against the open door. Bill was nowhere around. He tiptoed over to the desk to see that Bill had the MV document open. But Irma's folder contained a second file entitled 'Please read.' Horatio clicked on it.

'The Memetic Virus is untraceable and has the ability to adhere to whatever parameters are set for it. We have utilised several linguistic methods including NLP and subliminal messaging to reprogramme the human brain. This, combined with a microscopic second font, allows the MV can rewire the Subject's brain as per its designated program. For example, one could write the MV to make patients more open to charity or more respectful of authority. Some Subjects react to the virus violently while others shutdown entirely, symptoms are undetectable until it is too late. We lacked the foresight to develop a cure. The scope of this infection is vast and I would be remiss if I were not to mention the likely dangers it presents. I hereby request that further studies halt until we can draw fresh guidelines up. The other operators lack adequate training, each blinded by potential.'

He read and reread the missive, hoping he wasn't smart enough to understand what it was saying. But he knew what was happening, he'd exposed himself to the virus. Abraham, more than likely, had already released it to the public. It was too late. And then he remembered Abigail, her story, whatever hope they had of stopping a self-propagating virus would end if the photo reached print.

With a burst of energy, he leapt for the phone and called Abigail's number. Voicemail. He dialled again. Inside, he could feel a black ink spurt across his cortex, something eating away at his brain. The burrowing virus was impossible to resist, he had enough time to warn others. As he struggled to move his hands, he rang the paper's helpline. He imagined what he would tell them.

'Hello?' said a voice.

Horatio struggled to speak. He stared at the phone as whatever remnants of himself there still inside gave way the virus. It hurt as veins exploded. Tinnitus or static hummed over whispered yelps of unknown speaker. Overhearing murder, eyeing telephone. Horatio: 'I'm not…' Gasps.

The rest was silence.

The Prop Master, or
Rejected Submission #13

The cabin's windows shattered as two Molotov cocktails were hurled inside. Huddled together in the middle of the room, three co-eds, battered and bloody, begged for mercy. The fire made its way across the room engulfing all it touched. The corpses of the co-eds' friends lay scattered, waiting for their cremation. It would come in due time.

"Not like this, not like this!" Rebecca cried out.

"Oh god!" Tyrese agreed.

It was up to Bao, gorgeous but didn't know it, to save the day. "You're right, not like this. No way. We didn't come all this way to - to - oh shit, man this is really hot."

"CUT!"

Floodlights beamed in from outside the cabin. The cast's tortured faces became loose, relaxed, indifferent. Rebecca pulled a phone out from under a nearby sofa. Veronica the stunt coordinator rushed into the shot to turn off the fire. The room was just a room again.

"What is it this time?" Richard Hegel, Hollywood scion and self-styled guerrilla director stepped out from his hidden compartment followed closely by Bastion, the production's sole cameraman.

Bao flapped her hand like a dying bird and blew on it. "We're too close to the heat, H. Like way too close. I can't give a two-page monologue next to that fire, man, what the hell?"

"Are you seriously trying to talk to me about blocking right now? Blocking? This is supposed to feel, I don't know, *real*. Did that feel real to you? Do you even know what real is? You've blown the shot, you…" he paused. One more tweet about outbursts and even his lineage wouldn't save him from a decade of obscurity. "How long to reset the scene, Ron?"

Veronica looked at the broken windows and the singed carpets. "About an hour."

"Oh Christ, I hope you're all happy with yourselves. Do you think you'd make it in the golden years of horror?" Richard threw his clipboard to the ground and left the cabin. Outside was dark, the wind cold and biting, its fingers jabbed at the inside of the cabin for a moment before the door slammed itself shut.

The three talent stood in place as Bastion sat down and flipped through the shooting script and Veronica set about reconstructing the cabin. They were down to their last two panes of glass, she was mumbling to no one in particular.

"He's lucky I need this role," said Tyrese.

"Give him a break, this is his big vision," Rebecca said. She walked over to the blood-smeared mirror and straightened her clothing. They were their own continuity experts.

"Remaking *The Protocols of The Dead Gods* and setting it in a cabin? Did he even look at the source material? Talk about derivative. And he's going to lecture Bao about realness? Please. I'm glad this is the last day of filming." Tyrese sat down beside disembowelled wax figures of their slaughtered friends.

"But this movie is called *Winter Cabin of The Dead Ones 2: Terminal Prognosis,* I've never heard anything about dead goats," Rebecca said, happy her features had retained their synthetic bedraggledness.

"Dead Gods," Bao corrected. "Did you see it? The original?"

Bastion looked up from the script. "You know there was a play and a book at least before that first film."

"Either way," Bao replied, "Everyone involved in the first film died a mysterious death before the première. Only one person went to the cinema that night and they were found gutted and strung up from the Hollywood sign the following morning. It's a cursed film. Real dark blood cult stuff. "

Tyrese laughed as he walked over to the broken windows. "That's the rumour, anyway. But here's the thing: that film was set in a mortuary. The play and the book were both set in desolate seaside hotels. I don't know why Hegel even bothered, the jumped-up cretin."

Rebecca joined Tyrese by the window. Outside was darkness incarnate. The snow-covered floor shone like the darkest blue of a freshly turned off analogue television. There were trees out there. Warm cabins. A town with bars and people. "Just lay off the guy, this is his last shot at the big leagues. Even his old man has bailed on him. Besides, we just have to ham up this scene once and we're done. If Bao can quit being so soft for a second."

"How about you stand next to the fire next scene, then?" Bao asked.

"Because of continuity. I've always been in the middle."

"Honey, you've been wearing a different t-shirt every shot, I don't think he cares."

Veronica, who had lost herself to work, threw a hammer across the room. It all but embedded itself in the wall. Fortunately, just out of shot. "Well screw this, the fire machine needs a new valve."

The actors looked at her. They did not need to verbalise the "So?" but Rebecca said it anyway.

"So I need to go down the hill to Umberto for a replacement. Guy creeps me out. Please, Bastion, will you come with me?"

Bastion waved his shooting script in front of his face. "Can't do. Got to get this shot perfect if we want to get out of here in the morning."

Veronica looked at the actors. The two actresses suddenly found something interesting on their respective phones and disappeared into the cabin's bedrooms. "Well?"

Tyrese looked at the mannequins on the floor before closing his eyes and nodding. "Sure, can I get a coat first?"

"Only if you value your extremities."

Tyrese retrieved his jacket from underneath the battered remains of his character's dead fiancé. Even drenched in fake blood it possessed a certain charm. He would have to sneak it into his trailer after shooting ended.

Outside the two walked down the slope to the prop master's hut. It was a tiny star in the distance. Between them and it there was only darkness. They could feel the trees, hear the crunching of snow, see the spectral wisps of air escape their lungs. Something was watching them. The darkness was oppressive and dense and impenetrable. Even the light of Veronica's phone would get lost in the darkness. They walked as if on a tightrope suspended in the void toward the master's shack.

"So what is it about this guy you don't like? He seems pretty chill to me."

"That's exactly it. Don't you think there's something ghoulish about him? It's like talking to a stuffed corpse half the time. And those eyes. He never blinks. Just watch when we get there; the guy never blinks. Those black shark eyes just stare back at you like they want to eat your soul."

Tyrese shook his head.

"What?"

"Just, I wish we had lines like that in the film is all. You can tell Hegel wrote it himself, even if he is crediting some other writer. No way Benvolio Azhabphot is a real name."

"You do *not* like that man, do you?"

"Look, I spent fifteen years working tables and going to workshops before I got this role. I think I'm justified in disliking anyone who was born into success."

"If the shoe was on the other foot…"

"But it wasn't, though. That dude would have killed himself ten years ago if he had to endure half the stuff I've gone through."

"Preaching to the choir there. Oh, this walk gets longer every time I take it."

"Why is Umberto all the way down here anyway?"

"He likes his privacy. And Richy wants to keep his place out of shot, so it works out for all of us. The further away he is from me the better, man, I mean it. Don't leave me alone with him for even a second."

"Barring unforeseen circumstances I will protect you until the end."

Bao couldn't sit still. The holes where the windows were supposed to be were letting too much cold air in. The warmth from the fire had long since dissipated and the bedrooms were full of human flesh and bone. On top of which, Rebecca and Bastion were talking about their follow up movie Night Howl 7: The Return of Sanchez Panzer, an audition she remembered the way bitter, single men remember first dates that went nowhere.

"I'm just really excited to see the audience response when they find out the twist," Rebecca was saying.

"I'm trying to get them to let me do the whole thing in one continuous shot. Do you think that'd win any awards? I mean if that Freddie movie can win an Oscar for best editing I don't see why not, right?" Bastion was saying.

"Guys gotta go see Richard right quick. I'll be right back," said Bao. They didn't notice.

Outside was warmer than inside. Richard's trailer was hidden behind a wall of Douglas fir. She could see the faint shimmer of his porch light through the pines. Arms wrapped around herself like a madman in a straight jacket, she trundled toward the trees hoping to find the clearing but instead walked right through the branches until she reached the steps of Richard's trailer. The light above the door began to flicker as she approached it.

She didn't see it at first. His trailer was always a mess. Pizza boxes, cocaine residue, and whiskey bottles were strewn around. Enough to put a disgraced athlete to shame. But it was there all the same.

"Richard?" she whispered as she pushed the door open in increments. "Hegel? I need to talk about my monologue. Don't you think it would make more sense if I..."

There it was. Draped over the static-emitting television set. Richard's body -- his skin -- rested on the old box, white light buzzing through the membrane, his warped face looking back at her. In the bathroom, his insides dumped inside the bathtub, a trail of blood winding its way down from the light switch to the sink. Cabinet mirror smashed into pieces. Blood and gore and glass shards carpeted the bathroom floor and led out toward the television set.

And Bao screamed.

The Prop Master's cabin was warm and dimly lit. In any other circumstance, it would be considered romantic. But the countertops were littered with severed limbs and buckets of fake blood. Liszt was playing over cheap computer speakers, scratched and corrupted wav files from the days of dial-up connections and torrents. Umberto floated from room to room looking for a replacement valve.

"Yes," Umberto said, more a wheeze than a voice, "The valve is around here someplace if you'll just give me a moment. Veronica, would you like to help me look for it in this room?"

Tyrese and Veronica exchanged glances and Tyrese spoke. "We're just going to hang out in here, Umberto, if it's all the same to you. We have to get this last shot done before the sun starts to rise."

"The sun never rises," said Umberto, moving from one side room to another. It was at that moment Veronica noticed he wasn't walking, per se, but rather skittering across the floor. She nudged Tyrese who had noticed it too. Without noticing they were doing so, their bodies were inching toward both each other and the exit.

"The, uh, sun never rises?" said Veronica.

"No, no, the sun still always still. It is we who rise and fall and rise again and again and again like the teeter-totter doll of a child."

"Uh... if it's all the same to you, Umberto, could you just bring the valve up to the other cabin when you find it? We need to get back and--"

"Nonsense, I can never leave this place again. Never leave, never leave."

Umberto re-entered the living room and looked at his visitors. His flesh was hanging from his bones, his robe barely covering his torso. His black, unblinking eyes the one thing that seemed familiar, as small a blessing as that was. Phlegm rattled in his ribcage as he hovered over to the shelves and looked for the valve. His limbs moved as if the cartilage inside had been replaced by jelly. Veronica found herself missing the Umberto from the first day of the shoot; he may have been a casual misogynist with the mannerisms of an escaped serial killer, but at least his body wasn't rejecting itself back then.

Tyrese approached him and tried to help the search. "Don't, uh, don't prop masters usually keep everything in boxes?"

At this Umberto began to sob. It was the stifled, jagged sob of a child, one trying to explain what they wanted. He grasped onto Tyrese's shoulders and pulled him close.

"That… was… before… the… uh… oh… ugh…" Umberto said, his head tilting all the way back to reveal a swollen galaxy of blues and blacks wrapped around his throat, an injury far beyond simple bruising.

Veronica was already at the door and Tyrese was quick to join her. They were about to leave when

"Wait!" Umberto held something up for them to see. The valve. He surfed the floor toward them and handed it over the valve, grease smeared and warm, to Tyrese. And then he was gone. Disappeared into one of the smaller rooms. The lights turned off of their own accord and Veronica and Tyrese found themselves once more outside looking at a bright light off in the distance.

"Well you weren't lying about that guy," said Tyrese.

"It's probably just him and the prop master playing a joke on you," Bastion said. He walked with Bao back to Richard's trailer. Rebecca had stayed in the cabin, her contract specifically called for cocoa in the event of unscheduled trips outside and the cocoa had been gulped down hours earlier.

"I think I know real human flesh when I see it," said Bao.

"Oh, yeah, I forgot, you used to be a--"

"I know what I was. But the state of that room. Something happened in there. If was too hard to fake. Richard's dead, I just know it. You should be calling the police right now."

"Police aren't going to come out here after last time. You know that. Let's just make sure you saw what you think you saw before we make any rash decisions." The lingered outside the door, the light above is shone too brightly and popped inside the glass. Bastion fell backwards and landed hard on the ground beneath him. As he swore, the door flung open.

"Yes?" said Richard. "Is the cabin already reset? That's great."

"But…" Bao stared at the director. "You were skinned alive. Weren't you?"

"What is she talking about," Richard said to Bastion.

Bastion grunted as he got to his feet and limped to Bao's side. "Do you, uh, do you have a dead body in there or something?"

Richard chewed his tongue and stared off into the night sky. He began to hiss, then looked down at his visitors and laughed, wide-eyed and grinning. "Of course not, but come in real quick why don't you. I think I know what happened."

Bastion entered first. He let out a joyful laugh and looked back at Bao.

Bao looked beyond Bastion, beyond Richard and the inflatable sex toy he was claiming he'd left on the television, and into the trailer. The detritus was gone. The bathroom was clean, all human waste removed. But for a slither of brown sludge on the television screen, the room was immaculate. "No," said Bao, "You… there were pizza boxes in here. Cocaine. The bathroom had a--"

"So what is it? A dead body or pizza boxes? I know it can be very easy to confuse the two." Richard laughed again, more than he had the entire shoot, before tossing the deflated sex doll onto the couch. He entered the bathroom and began to examine his face. "If you must know, yes, this room was a bit messy because I relapsed the other day. I'm better now though. Although I did cut myself shaving this morning, hence all the blood you saw. But I promise I am completely house trained most of the time."

Bastion smiled and nodded along, nudging Bao as he did so. Then he froze. Something was grinding against Richard's spine, underneath his t-shirt. A thick serpentine mass was flailing under the surface, pulsating like an additional lung. Bao noticed it too. She was about to speak when Bastion placed a finger against his lips and bulged his eyes.

"Yes, you'd have thought I would be able to shave after all these years, but there we go. I'm sorry if I freaked you out earlier, Bao. And sorry for my outburst after your scene. We'll turn the fire down next time and add extra in post if we have to."

Bao tried to appear gracious. Her acting chops, or lack thereof, almost betrayed her. Richard was too focused on invisible crumbs on the floor to notice. He was cleaning up still, although cleaning nothing either Bastion or Bao could see. Even Bastion's DSLR camera with the 1000x zoom would have had a hard time seeing what Richard could see.

"Well," Bastion said, making a quick scoot toward the door, "We'll be in the cabin when you're ready to shoot."

He left without waiting for a response. Bao was quick to follow.

"Where's Rebecca?" Veronica asked as she entered the cabin. Bao and Bastion were pacing across the room, near catatonic, and did not hear.

"Hey, where's Rebecca?" Tyrese echoed.

Bao stopped and looked at them. Through them. She back off toward the furthest wall and pointed at them. "Turn around," she said. "Turn around and lift up your shirts."

Veronica shook her head. "Yeah, we're not doing that. Something's off about the prop master even for him, so if we could just get this shot done I'm just going to head into town for the night. There's got to be a hotel down there."

She moved the flammable rig and began to reattach the valve, ignoring the others.

Tyrese saw the panic in Bao's eyes and turned, lifting up his back. Bao sighed, relieved. Bastion did the same. "Now, you mind telling me what this is all about?" Tyrese said.

Bao looked down, not fully believing what she was about to say, "I don't think Richard is Richard any more."

"What does that mean?"

"I saw his flesh. Saw his bones in the sink. There was blood everywhere. And then there wasn't. I, god, man, I don't know."

Bastion stood beside her, planting a tender palm on her shoulder. "He had something growing on his back. It was like, I don't know…"

"Like he wasn't fully human?" Tyrese asked. "I got the same vibe from Umberto. His throat was all bruised and I don't think he was walking. Floating. Like a hundred centipede legs were carrying him from room to room."

Veronica came up from under the rig. "All the more reason to go find a hotel. But whatever is going on, if they know we know, we're done for."

Bao was jolted by a realisation. "Rebecca. Shit. Where is she? We need to find her. Why couldn't she just stay put?"

"I'll go look for her," said Tyrese. "I think she trusts me."

"She told me she thinks you're a dick, but yeah, let's just go, we'll be better as a team," said Bao. "Are you two coming?"

Veronica shook her head. "There's light in here and if Richard comes back I want to see him coming."

"Bastion?"

"If the lady's staying, I can't leave her alone."

"Very noble of you," said Veronica.

"Hardly," Bastion sneered, "I don't want us coming back here and find you changed is all."

"Ah, so smart."

Tyrese and Bao left through the back door. They could not have seen Richard standing beside the broken window at the front of the cabin.

They walked into the woods for what felt like an hour but was closer to five minutes. It was a muted walk, like even the wind and the animals had run away. The black walls of trees loomed over them, motionless and oppressive. They found Rebecca in a clearing. She turned to face them, illuminated for a moment as the moon broke through the clouds. She was smiling, dressed in white, her whole body glowed as she acknowledged them.

"I was looking for you," she said to them.

"You'd have found us a lot faster if you'd have waited in the cabin," Bao replied.

"No, I needed to get out of there." Darkness again, the moon lost to the vapours.   "It's sort of a woman problem. Bao, can we talk about it for a minute in private."

Bao stepped forward but felt Tyrese's hand against her chest, holding her back.

"How do we know you're the real you?" he said.

"What are you talking about?"

"Something's going on. Why don't we all go back to the cabin and we'll talk there, OK?"

Rebecca giggled. "Oh no, that will not do, I'm afraid. It cannot wait. I must tell you now."

The moon returned in full force. Rebecca was not standing, she was floating a foot above the ground. Blood flowed down her legs and pooled on the reddening snow beneath her. A warped and pulsing something protruded from her back and disappeared into the woods behind her. She was smiling.

"Just over here, please, Bao, it's super girly what I need to tell you," the thing pretending to be Rebecca said its voice breaking. "Please Bao. Please, Bao. Please, Bao. Please, Bao. Please--"

Tyrese was already running, Bao was fast behind him.

"I guess you're probably pretty tough if you're a stunt coordinator, right?"

"And?"

"Just... I think if it comes down to it we should know who can hold their own. I did two tours of Cyprus so I know I can handle myself. Not sure about the actors. I guess I'm saying it may come down to the two of us if they don't come back."

"Were we ever at war with Cyprus?"

"Why does that matter?"

Richard entered the room. "Hey guys, are we ready guys? Are we ready? Where are my actors? I need my actors."

Bastion picked up his tripod. "They're, uh, they're outside taking a smoke."

"Yeah," Veronica agreed. "We'll go get them for you if you want."

Richard stepped on the scorched part of the floor and clucked. "We know you know. You will feel so much better if you join us. Let us inside you, please."

His back tore open and three tentacles uncoiled, lashing up and out in search for their prey. "Just stand still. It will be over in a second."

Veronica noticed where Richard was standing and dove for her rig. The fire erupted, but it was too late. Richard had stepped away from the flame and was slowly unravelling, a mass of bubonic tendrils whirling out of him. His face, looking like a warped wax figurine melting under the sun, looked at her, his eyes were gone, replaced with glowing black orbs. "SooooOOOooooon," he cackled.

Bastion was quick to open the tripod and surged toward Richard, pushing him into the roaring fire. Richard's interloper howled in agony as the old flesh seared and bubbled under the heat.

Bastion smiled, he turned to face Veronica and said "See, I to--" only for a tentacle to lash out from the inferno and wrap around his neck. Veronica rushed to grab his hand, to pull him to safety, but it was too hot, the tentacle too strong, and he was pulled into the flame. Veronica fell to her knees as a hundred voices screamed out in agony amongst the pops and sizzles of the combustible floor.

They could see a shadow up above the trees as they ran back to the cabin. "Please Bao, Please Bao" it continued to scream as it swooped down trying to touch them. They zigzagged through pine and didn't look back until they were inside the cabin. Rebecca's puppeteer landing on the roof and stomped on the tiles.

Before them, they saw Veronica curled up on the floor as flamed lapped up a mangled wreck of limbs and flesh. Whatever it was twitched, continued to twitch, as is blustered and bubbled and died.

"Richard," Veronica explained. "Richard and… oh man, Bastion. He tried to, tried to stop it. Stupid. Stupid."

Bao stepped forward to comfort her but once again felt Tyrese's hand on her chest.

"She's been left alone. We don't know if that's the real Veronica or not."

"Guys, why would a fake Veronica burn Richard up."

Tyrese contemplated this. "To throw us off the scent, maybe."

At this, the baked remains of Richard's inside began to slither and pop as Bastion's charred corpse sat up. Its one remaining eye opened, its jaw, held connected to the rest of the head by a thread, began to move. "Guys, I'm OK, everything is fine. She's with me, OK? You can trust her."

"Yesssssssss," Richard's voice hissed from inside the wreckage. "You're safe now."

"No, no, no," Tyrese said, backing up to the read window.

Bao fell to her knees and crawled next to Veronica, checking her for markings. "We have to go. We have to go now, head straight for the town. This is our only chance. Tyrese, help me get her up and… no!"

Rebecca's hands had clawed their way through Tyrese's stomach. He looked down with considerable disbelief as he was pulled through the window and out into the darkness.

Veronica needed no encouragement to stand. She and Bao ran to the front door but were greeted by Umberto. Dark bile trickled down his chin and his onyx eyes rolled backwards in his eyes. "Where are you going?" he said.

"Yes, where?" said Bastion.

"Yessssssssssss," said Richard.

"Please Bao," said Rebecca from outside.

"Splguhsuhsurgh," said Tyrese.

Back to back, the two women walked to the centre of the room. They linked armed and braced for the worst. "Why," said Bao, "Why did we have to remake a classic film about Az Habphot and set it in a cabin? When will people learn to let the dead gods of old rest? Why do they summon them onto this plane to feed and destroy the very essence of life itself? Why? Why? Why?"

"CUT!" the director called from his hidden compartment. It opened the door and revealed itself. The camera followed.

Bao shook her head. "What is it? Did I say the wrong thing?"

"No, you read it perfectly sweety, it's just…"

"What?"

"A little too on the nose, don't you think? It's the final scene of the film. We don't want people thinking they just left an afternoon special."

Veronica's vile mass of tortured limbs left her fleshy costume and walked. A levitating ball of pure hatred and anger made its way to the door. "Sweetie, if you feel like doing rewrites, I'm just going to be outside, is that OK?"

"Whatever you need to do, Baas Ek Slaoth. It won't take long. We just need to trim it down. Maybe add a few lines into earlier scenes to hammer the message home."

A skeletal assortment of teeth and pustules leaned in from outside, Tyrese's flesh flung over its shoulder. "If you want, I can go dub some lines now. I won't be around for post-production, you know."

"Oh yeah," said Bao, "You've got that thing with the--"

"Sleepy coastal town in Maine, yeah. It's a big break for me."

The director nodded. "Right, you go just feed some lines in. Just bring up Az Habphot and the curse of The Protocols movie, or something. I mean you're the co-writer, so you know what you're doing. "

The skeleton gave a glib salute and disappeared into the night.

"I've got it!" Bao said. "Could we just cut to black when we're surrounded and then fade to the premier? Like a subtle reference like that?"

"We'd have to find the location. But we still have you for what--"

"A week."

"Then let's try and make that work. Maybe fade out to some VO while we're at it?"

"See, that's why you're the director."

"Could I make a suggestion?" the burnt mass of carnage on the floor asked.

"Yeah, go for it, Tony."

"What if we end with Bao back in her car going to the audition. She could tell Richard the whole project is cursed and he could be all, like, yeah, I know."

"I love it but I don't think we have time for that."

"No problem, my dude, just an idea."

The director bounced up and down. Creative juices flowed and got It amped up. Az Habphot the invisible and immortal puppeteer, Its hundred thousand limbs skittered through a thousand times and dimensions and controlled them all. In the night It whispered and consorted and recruited, always recruited. An uncountable army of beings at Its command, always waiting, always dancing toward oblivion. A roving mass of chaos itself, Az Habphot surveyed the shooting site and smiled a smiled which would turn a mortal man into a raving loon, for Its mouth was a whole in the universe itself. Finally, a film that would ear his kind the respect it deserved. And the viewers would have no choice because Az Habphot's tendrils would claim the eyes of all who saw him.

"Guys, I'm going to go get some coffee if anyone wants something," said Umberto the prop master.

"Yes," said Bao, "Pick up some stray dogs and a child for me."

The pile on the floor writhed. "I'll take some sour candy and a new lighter and a lonely man."

Umberto nodded. "The usual then. I'll be right back."

Az Habphot needed nothing but all of time and space. And a few close-ups of Bao while they waited.

Minutes from a White Nationalist Meeting

OPENING

The third meeting for United Europeans for New American Country was called to order at 7:38 PM on Wednesday the 27th of August 2025 at the Arby's on Washington Avenue by Steve Blumfeld.

PRESENT

Thor Hitler Rand (*Chairman*); Odin Hitler Galt (*Vice-Chairman*); Steve Blumfeld (*Treasurer*); Roger Dangerous (*Grand Inquisitor*); James Oakley (*Grand Dragon*); Ben "GenoSide88" Sharpton (*YouTube Personality and Philosopher*); Brick "xXxmemetankxXx" Larson (*Twitch Streamer and Philosopher*); Doctor Chester Cobblepots MFA (*Classical Liberal Pundit and Philosopher); Titan Oberon Spigot III (*Financier and Online University Faculty and Philosopher*).

APPROVAL OF AGENDA

Agenda was approved unanimously as distributed.

APPROVAL OF MINUTES

The minutes of the previous meeting were categorically rejected on the grounds that Item 2 of the previous meeting (i.e.: "replace all racial slurs with ironic memes and winky face emojis") rendered the entire transcript unreadable. Item 2's approval has retroactively been redacted retroactively.

OPEN ISSUES

1.   **Name for New Country** – Each member of the new country has proposed their own idea for a name and as such our new great country is still nameless. Proposal for second referendum to be revisited at a later date.

2.   **Recruitment of Women** – There is still concern over the ratio of men and women in our great new sovereign nation. Motion to invite noted Twitter pundits enter the country regardless of ethnic background or religious affiliation was denied by a 3:1 margin because, quote, "Even we don't want that crazy around us."

3.   **Workers** – As per nation's charter, all citizens have been allowed to self-determine their roles in this great and wonderful city. However, 90% of all residents have decided to become Freethinking Free Speech Internet Activists, with the other 10% divided evenly between "Professional Gamer" and "CGI Expert Who Takes all the Black People and Women out of Films They Like." As such, there is a complete lack of personnel in the following fields: all of them. Members have been asked to provide ideas on how to fix this issue. Three proposals have been submitted and will be voted upon at the next meeting. They are:

A)   **Fresh IQ tests for all residents** – Proposed by Roger Dangerous (IQ 178) and seconded by Doctor Chester Cobblepots MFA (estimated IQ 239). As the majority of our Great Nation's residents put their IQ somewhere between 150 and 165, fresh tests would allow the less intelligent to work in factories. "Where they belong," to quote Roger.

B)   **DNA tests for all residents** – Proposed by Odin Hitler Galt and seconded by Titan Oberon Spigot III. Residents with more DNA from England (not Wales, Scotland, or Northern Ireland) or Western Europe (not including Spain, Portugal, or Italy), would be given preferential treatment in the country. Some contention here from others present as they all argue their region of origin is "more white." Chairman Thor Hitler Rand rules in favour of Odin Hitler Galt as their ancestors are all from London and it "just makes sense."

C)   **Hire minorities to do all the work** – proposed by Brick Larson and seconded by a woman at a nearby table. Brick argues that this would allow all our Citizens an equal chance to own the libs with hilarious critique videos and memes.

NEW BUSINESS

1.   **Concern re: Thor Hitler Rand's attire** – Ben Sharpton is concerned that the chairman's ensemble (a stormtrooper uniform and a Klansman hood) might be considered racist by neighbouring countries. Thor points out that it's "just a joke, bro," which is enough to alleviate Ben's complaints. Ben reminds us that he's just asking questions and definitely isn't triggered.

2.   **Misc. Comments concerning the word "Triggered"** – Attendees laugh about how triggered other countries are for fifty minutes. Order fresh round of burgers and soda.

3.   **Food shortages** – James Oakley brings up the fact our Great Unnamed Nation has no real food. Odin points out that so long as neighbouring countries have fast food, everything is fine.

4.   **Snack Break** – Brick's mother cooked tamales and samosas for everyone.

5.   **Potential Treaty with nearby sovereign nation** – The lowly nation of Musktopia has proposed a peace treaty and trade pact. Roger Dangerous votes against as he is in the middle of a Twitter spat with Musktopia's Emperor. Steve Blumfeld votes for as he needs a new car. Referendum to be held at future date.

6.   **National Anthem** – Several anonymous civilians have pointed out that Our Great Nation's Anthem was written by a gay, black Jew. Not that there's anything wrong with that, wink. Motion passed to change national anthem. Ain't No Mountain proposed as new anthem. Motion unanimously passed.

7.   **Concerns re: racism** – noting his Twitch stream and his fears of being deplatformed, Brick asks for the third meeting in a row for assurances the whole "ethnostate" thing isn't as racist as some of his fans are saying. Concerns allayed by everyone in attendance saying "no, no, of course not!" and winking at each other. Winks, of course, being Our Wonderful Nation's sign of respect and honesty.

AGENDA FOR NEXT MEETING
1.   **Current Business**
2.   **Ideas for new flag that don't involve racist iconography, or else a plausible argument for why racist iconography is good, actually**
3.   **Recruitment drive for nation's military**
4.   **Deciding on which Test-booster is Our Great Nation's Official Supplement**
5.   **Child Pornography: How much is too much?**
6.   **Declaring war on neighbouring LGBT+ country as a meme, wink.**

7.   Anime, or; Why Japanese People Should Be Considered White, Please

8.   The Jewish Question: How to watch Friends without any scenes including Ross and Monica

9.   Showers and Laundry: What are they? And why should we care?

ADJOURNMENT

Meeting was adjourned at 11:59PM by Steve Blumfeld. The next general meeting will be at 15:30 on Wednesday 4th of September, in Dre's Pizzeria and Ball Pit (bring money for tokens).

Minutes Submitted by: Steve Blumfeld
Approved by: Steve Blumfeld

The Cop Who Died and Became a Skeleton and Wanted Spicy Bean Burritos

(Note: This story was originally featured in award-winning, paradigm shifting, literary behemoth Taco Bell Quarterly)

Imagine yourself naked. Got it? Good. Now imagine all of your skin and your muscles and your insides were gone. Still with me? Great! What you're imagining is roughly how Detective Hector Boniface PhD looks like on a good day. i.e. he is a skeleton. That is, a skeleton cop with a PhD in cosmetology, to be precise.

Now, I've already made a mistake, because when I said "imagine yourself naked" I should have said "imagine yourself wearing some really badass jeans and a leather duster jacket and, like, a vintage Hawaiian shirt, but not one of those gaudy ones you see in tourist spots. Oh! And also a cool trilby and a nice pair of aviator shade. Not too nice, though. Aviator shades that were found in a thrift store back before thrift stores started charging as much as most other stores. And what's up with that anyway? Do they not know what a thrift store is supposed to be?" Because Detective Hector Boniface PHD would never get naked. Why would he? It's not like he has reproductive organs – any organs, really – or, like, a really sick tattoo of a pair of dragons on his back. Because you can't tattoo skeletons. Believe me. And besides which, if Detective Hector Boniface PHD doesn't wear his completely killer ensemble his bones might fall apart and he'd become a pile of bones on the ground. And that would just be ridiculous. Where do you think this is? Thirteen feet beneath Paris?

Now, I may have gotten a little sidetracked here, but the important things to remember as I tell this completely true story is that:

A) Hector is a skeleton

B) Hector has the coolest taste in clothes, and everyone is impressed and intimidated by him, as much because of his outfit as they are by the fact he's an inhuman abomination of walking bones

C) Skeletons don't have sex so please don't ship my original character and help generate interest in future Detective Hector Boniface PhD stories, because I would hate that. Please. No Hector Boniface x Jeff the Killer. No Hector Boniface x Dad. No Hector Boniface x Everyone from that Netflix show. Please. And don't even think about getting that Reigns YouTuber or whoever to do an "Is Detective Hector Boniface PHD real?" video. Don't do any of that. I am demanding you not to do any of that. Please. The publicity and demand on my time would be a huge inconvenience, and I am telling you not to do it.

So, but, anyway, Hector Boniface was driving up and down Wisconsin Avenue for almost three hours while he waited for the Taco Bell to open. He had been jonesing for some spicy bean burritos for months and was finally able to make his dream a reality after his reanimated remains came back to life. Taco Bells were surprisingly hard to come across in South-Eastern Wisconsin. There was that one on the interstate near Racine and the one on North, but the one on Wisconsin Avenue was where it was at. They always gave him extra hot sauce back before he had his accident and lost all his tissue and musculature.

Oh, by the way, for those reading this, Hector drove a 1973 Plymouth Volare with a custom muffler and tinted windows, the sort that made everything look dark but not too dark. He was just that kind of cop when he was alive; a maverick cop who played by his own rules and liked to live on the edge right up to and including his fatal and horrific accident that took all his skin and fatty acids and hair away. Some people say that kind of car isn't as manly as a Mustang or Cobalt, and that people who drive obscure, modified old muscle cars are overcompensating for their own subconscious feelings of alienation and inadequacy in an increasingly solipsistic society, but those people can go fuck themselves, Paul.

The drive thru of the Taco Bell on Wisconsin Avenue already had a car in the line when Hector finished his final loop of the road. He was angry at his lack of patience. Maybe for the best, though, he reasoned. Perhaps waiting would give the food inside more time to get warm.

The car ahead moved forward to the next window.

"Hello, this is Taco Bell," said a speaker.

"Yes, this is Detective Hector Boniface PHD and I would like five fiery hot bean burritos. I'm talking yo soy muy caliente y como el fuego del sol, por favor and thank you."

"Uh… five spicy bean burritos? Anything else?"

"Yes, I would like a big soda."

"What?"

"A big soda."

"I heard. What kind."

"Surprise me."

Huge sighs from the window. "Next window please."

Hector pulled up to the next window. He took out his alligator skin wallet and got ready to pay. Some of his old friends from back before he got drunk and removed the pia mater – and, for that matter, the rest of his mater from his bones – used to drag him for having an alligator skin wallet. "Oh, that's really cruel and pointless, having one of those," one of them would say. "At least people eat the cows they get leather from, you've never eaten gator in your life," they would yell at him in the changing rooms of the police department. "What are you, a seventy-year-old trucker from Louisiana who thinks buying all their clothes from beer suppliers and motorbike manufacturers makes up for your complete lack of personality?" But, actually, alligator skin wallets are really cool and anybody who disagreed probably has something wrong with them in the personality and looks departments.

"We can't serve you," the person at the window of the Taco Bell said.

"Why not? I've got money."

"You're dead."

"I'm undead."

"What's the difference?"

"The difference is I want those five spicy bean burritos I just ordered."

"I will have to ask the manager. Can you pull over there, please?"

"Fine, but I better get my five spicy bean burritos and big drink of soda."

A heavy sigh. Hector moved his car over to the empty spot. The people behind him were served just fine. The street had been worked on since he'd last looked at it, but it was an odd kind of neighbourhood. Yes, very odd indeed. An eclectic mix of residents. You wouldn't get that anywhere else in Milwaukee, just as you might as well not get any Taco Bell anywhere else in Milwaukee. Imagine driving all the way to Racine to get some tasty 3AM burritos and then stopping in at a friends bar that's not supposed to still be open but is. Imagine that. Imagine sitting in the closed bar, knowing full well they're breaking the law, and then deciding to go break into a nearby firework store with your burritos and top shelf vodka and accidentally blowing yourself up. Blowing yourself up so much that you're thrown into the air and plummet right into the way of a county operated snow plow and having your burning flesh torn off your bones, never getting to enjoy the rest of those tasty late night Taco Bell burritos. And let's be honest, as far as burritos go they're pas mal, but as edible spicy bean-based goodness in affordable, biodegradable wrapping? They're up there with the best. Deep-fried cheese curds, deep-fried candy bars, bell pepper Cajun fries, Taco Bell spicy bean burritos. That was the holy Quadrumvirate right there. Yes sir. And yet, of all of those foods, somehow, it was getting his hands on the succulent, flaming goodness, those squelchy corn flour sacks of goodness, that proved the most difficult.

In all honesty, he should have just driven down to the Oasis just south of Waukegan, because they never closed and probably wouldn't say no to a skeleton, either. But then there's the whole hassle of Illinois tolls and the 10% tax and… you know.

Hector saw the manager come out. As Taco Bell managers went, they looked about the same as he'd expected. Largely because he remembered the manager from the last time he was there.

"Are you the skeleton asking about the spicy burritos?" the manager asked.

"Yes, is that a problem?" he was worried when he said that because it sounded more confrontational than he expected.

"If it was a problem you would know about it. Listen, we're not supposed to give our burritos to the undead any more, but for you I can make an exception. You have to eat in the car, though, understand?"

"That's why I used the drive through."

"Yes, but we don't want you eating it out in public down by the library or something. If the undead Marquette students find out we served you, we'll never hear the end of it. And I probably mean that literally."

"Thank you for being so understanding."

"Don't mention it. My grandma is a wraith, but you know how corporate policy can be."

Hector did know how corporate policy could be. The Collectivo coffee shop on the lake front wouldn't serve him coffee any more after his hand fell off and he burnt that guy. Persona non grata, they said. Latin made Hector's skin boil. Skin? Made something boil, at any rate.

The manager returned with a nondescript bag full of spicy bean burritos. It felt closer to seven or eight burritos and some extra condiments. You could always rely on the Wisconsin Avenue Taco Bell, that was for sure. He brought the surprised drink out, too. From the looks of it, whoever made it inside had mixed the cherry cola with the lemonade. Perfect. What a great day.

"What a great day," said Hector. "How much do I owe you?"

"Oh, don't worry about it. It's on the house. But you must promise never to come back here, please."

Hector nodded. He preferred the one near Racine anyway.

The manage returned to the Taco Bell and Hector opened up his bag. So nice to finally have a chance to taste the spicy goodness again. It had been too long. Far too long. He had waited what felt like a life time to get to eat more burritos. And finally. And finally.

Hector unwrapped the first of his burritos and took a giant bite. He couldn't taste anything. He had no papillae, after all. No matter. He was chewed on the healthy serving and swallowed. Nothing. He could sense the food falling down through his ribcage and onto his really expensive and cool jeans. He took another bite. The same thing. In the end, the burritos all went straight through him like nothing and wound up on the seat of his car. Same as it ever was. He thought he'd wash it all down with his mystery soda and remembered too late he was a skeleton. The contents cascaded down through his skeletal frame, soaking his clothes and ruining his newly reupholstered seat. Red soda seeping through his ribs, his teeth, pouring down his ribs like that scene from the Shining. It got all over his very impressive car. All over.

And that's why they don't serve skeletons at Taco Bell.

Elite Survival

The purple whisper of a fading day crept beyond the horizon, shrinking into the past like so many before it as torpid clouds overhead pulsed with impending darkness. A pair of hands foraged through the dirt as what remained of the light began to dissipate. Faint flickers of fire far across the barren field helped a little. Another fire would have been even more helpful, but it had taken them three days just to get the first one going. And so, the hands searched with increasing desperation, like a nervous citizen looking for their passport at a checkpoint.

Nothing. The hands could find nothing.

The outcome, in each case, was death. One slow, the other mercifully fast.

Up until that morning, Johnstone Blythe Seaton-Sminkerton III was certain he had grown a bountiful harvest. Vegetables and fruits of all shapes and sizes growing fastidiously beneath the earth, thanks to months of his unrelenting farming prowess. After all, his family had owned huge swathes of farmland for generations, ever since they betrayed one monarch for another, so the earth was in his blood. He was basically one of those Natives he'd heard about on the radio, but with more land and a knighthood.

And yet, poor Johnstone Blythe Seaton-Sminkerton III had only been able to produce one small carrot. A single orange runt. It must have been someone else's fault, he was sure, because he was incapable of making a mistake. Mummy had told him as much for the first sixty years of his life. "The Seaton-Sminkertons do not make mistakes," she would say, "Now get out of my bed and go back to work."

The carrot dangled, impaled on metal rod, bobbing above the fire. One side of the carrot had become black and was beginning to ooze bubbling, white liquid which hissed against the glowing ambers beneath. Sir Samael Jones-Blisphsthby Balderdash had been holding the carrot over the fire for three hours and could not understand how it had yet to get soft in the middle – the universal sign of a food's readiness. It was probably a bad carrot, he thought to himself. After all, he had served as a chef aboard a naval vessel for almost three whole weeks before his grandfather relented and made him an admiral.

If a common layman could cook a carrot, then it stood to reason Sir Samael would have no problems whatsoever. He had never been wrong, never failed in his life. Even living in a manor full of dead people, he was one of the few capable and competent enough not to have succumbed to dying. So surely, he thought, surely it was the carrot's fault for not cooking properly. Or else it was the fault of the fatuous Johnstone and his third-rate command of Latin.

And yet the carrot remained stiff and burned and leaking. He stared at it as if his eyes could convince it to change, as they had changed so many minds in the years before the calamity. The calamity had ruined everything.

From inside the manor, Lord Dmitri Rusev Blancho-Guttenberg watched the cretinous nobility outside. One hunched over the small fire, the other dancing into the shadows in a foolish attempt to find food he hadn't been able to create. Lord Dmitri Rusev Blancho-Guttenberg – Ed Smith to his constituents – hated what remained of their group. And where had the fourth one run off to? He strummed his finger on the glass, thinking dark thoughts only a born leader could summon into existence. *They were going to eat the food without him.* He just knew it.

It paid to be paranoid when you were a man of Dmitri's stock. He had warned the general public of the dangers of invading immigrants, and he'd have probably been proven right if the cataclysm hadn't occurred so soon into his reign. It stood to reason they would eventually start evading taxes and manipulating the law to their own end and covering up various heinous crimes against young children, because that's what *his* family had been doing since they arrived in England three hundred years ago. He was right to warn of the growing civil unrest and death, too. His only mistake – and he was at loath to call it a mistake because he, too, had an aversion to the concept – was assuming the oligarchs had room for him in their bunkers and spaceships. They did not. Instead, Dmitri was forced to stay in England with the lesser people, most of whom incorrectly blamed him for their problems. How was he to know that taking people's food, money, shelter, sense of importance, health, community, and US-made sitcoms would be so detrimental to society? A little tough love had never steered him wrong.

If they didn't want to starve to death, they shouldn't have been poor in the first place.

Speaking of starving to death, he began to canter outside toward the field before the food was stolen from him. He paused with reverence against the door leading to the west wing. Through the door, one hundred or so of his closest friends lay in varying states of decay. Most hadn't made it through the first winter, convinced as they were of their own rugged masculinity. They smoked cigars and drank scotch, after all, and what else did a man need to do to become tough? The slower to die stole brandy supplies and drank themselves dead, or stopped eating, or simply found a world without servants was one they were incapable of living in and obligingly stopped doing so.

The east wing was not much better. No longer a manor, then, but a mausoleum for great men, perhaps the last great men of the country, all gone before their time. The four remaining men would have had a lot more room if they tossed out the corpses, but none of them wanted to. It was a job for the janitorial class. The janitorial class were probably all dead, Dmitri thought, and so the corpses would remain in the manor until they disappeared into the wooden floors beneath them or were eaten by the rats Johnstone had been unable to catch.

"You better not be eating all the food without me," Dmitri began, looming over the fire like a frail demon.

"No, prime minister, one would simply not dream of it," said Samael. "It's just taking longer to cook than expected."

"What are we eating this evening anyway?"

"Well, prime minister, we only have the one carrot today."

"Hell's teeth!" Dmitri exclaimed. He knew they should have rationed out the supplies they'd borrowed from the neighbouring influencer camp. "I should have it. I am prime minister after all."

Samael looked at him. "That's only a title, though, isn't it, sir? I mean, Dmitri."

"Please, call me Ed. And give me the carrot."

"Ed, as I was saying, please don't interrupt me, sir, was there's not really a country to govern anymore and besides which, I am the one who cooked the carrot."

The dark mass of Johnstone waddled into the faint orange glow and coughed. "I grew the thing. If we're not sharing it, I am entitled to the whole carrot."

"You should get nothing for being unable to grow a whole crop."

"Maybe if I had some help."

"We agreed to our roles months ago, man. I'm the chef, you're an inept farmer, and Dm—Ed is whatever he pretends he's doing at the time."

An argument began.

William Maypole had been foraging through the underbrush of the manor's perimeter before he returned. He was depressed but not shocked to see an argument had begun. Three men, each convinced of their own superiority, arguing over a ruined carrot. Screaming until they got their own way was something they learned before they could walk, but they truly peaked in the last years of the country, when everything was falling apart. Arguing was the last remnant of their old life, even while their friends and alleged constituents lay dying in the streets they argued. The thing with arguing was, it was a war of attrition not of intellect, and only a select few knew that secret. Most who knew the secret lay dead in the halls of the manor behind them.

His pace slowed as the three men began to gesture wildly at the carrot and each other. There was only one thing that could come from the debate, an old tactic learned in childhood William had been fortunate to avoid thanks to overseas schooling. He stopped walking entirely, hidden by the darkness, and waited. Soon, one of his three colleagues would possibly yell something out. If they *did* yell that something out, William knew it was time to leave. No food, three idiots, and their combined two centuries of private school and familial abuse had rendered his time in the manor a walking nightmare.

"Right!" Dmitri yelled, on a cue he couldn't possibly have known about, "Wanky bum-bum it is!"

The three men standing around the fire loosened their already ill-fitting pants and dropped them to their ankles. William turned. It was not a game he could watch again. For a moment, he was glad of his education in Dubai. For a moment. Then came the realisation that he had to leave the manor. They would all be dead soon, and he couldn't – refused – to spend his remaining days watching the Old Boys Network try to solve their pointless debates through questionable hazing rituals. He turned and walked to the front gate. There had to be another way.

Outside the manor, the ground was covered in the shadowed remains of the dead. Even in the descending nightfall, William knew them all. They had waited, obligingly, outside the manor, hoping those inside would take pity on them, let them in, save them as they had promised so many times to do, reward their loyalty. Every single one of them died just as the disillusionment hit. Kate Epcott was the first to go. Her body still dangled from a branch near the gate. While she had sold her journalistic integrity out in her late twenties, she still had it inside her somewhere, dormant, waiting. As the manor gates closed on her face, she knew her complicit nature wasn't enough to save her. Burt Reinbach died of a heart attack soon after. He had two photos of him standing beside billionaires. He was a regional manager before the end. This couldn't save him. Nathan Prescott starved to death holding Dmitri's manifesto. His loyalty couldn't save him.

William tried to look forward as he tiptoed over their decaying husks. He knew they were there, and he had betrayed them. Eliza Bartholomew's crass indifference didn't save her. John Sibyl's online persona couldn't save him. Clare Steinbach's pithy comedy career was never going to save her as anti-PC as it was. Richard Pate's ignorance hadn't been enough to save his life. Elmira Kudzu's hundred thousand racist subscribers meant absolutely nothing to those who could have let her in. Duncan Teapot's role as a devil's advocate didn't stop the diphtheria, the anguished cries alone in the dark with no help to be found. Winston Brooks spent his life convinced selling out his working-class roots would somehow grant him immortality, and his desiccated, warped corpse lay as evidence to the contrary. A hundred or so bodies all told the same story; one of fatal disappointment. William had to navigate through their huddled remains, people convinced they would be granted mercy by old men who did not know or care they existed, or indeed understand the meaning of the word mercy. William would have cried if crying hadn't been beaten out of him in his youth.

He walked like a ghoulish John Cleese (coincidentally, also dead), and looked around him. The fire a dim spot in the distance; the argument over the carrot little more than a murmur. In all other directions only darkness and death. At least no Wanky Bum-Bum, he thought. At least no old men convinced of their own greatness and oblivious to their own failings, no futile wasted days of silent desperation, no nights in chilly manors full of dead people too proud to know the end had found them. William thought of one some Buddhist book or another, one an old girlfriend bought him back when his girlfriends bought gifts, and how it would talk about oblivion. Oblivion. It was the best alternative. Because what else was there? The cities were overrun, barracks overrun with fitness models and amateur rappers, even the other manors had become abattoirs of short-sighted greed and anger. There was nowhere left to go. Except maybe the north, William thought.

He walked east.

He crossed over broken roads and meadows for what felt like the entire night but was in fact forty-five minutes. Stopping, he turned again, looked back at where he thought the manor would be. Nothing. He was looking in the wrong direction. William's feet were swollen, knees sore, lower back a bit numb. Sweat formed on his brow, his armpits musty, breath short, inclination to keep going minimal. William decided to take a nap.

It wouldn't be the first time he had slept rough. He once slept rough in Edinburgh for one night because the Trainspotting guy was reading on stage and it was for charity. Of course, he left after the Trainspotting guy stopped reading and checked into the nearest hotel, but the intent had been there. He'd slept rough more than most, he reasoned.

Of course, sleeping rough alone in a field in the middle of nowhere is a horse of a different pallet, and he lay there exhausted but nervous, half-asleep but with the alertness of the truly paranoid, until the sun returned once more. Limbs creaking, stomach beyond empty, eyes wishing to rebel against him in so many ways. Sleeping in a field without a tent, especially when you don't *want* to be sleeping in a field, is not sleep at all, but rather a roving series of waking nightmares. If only someone had told him sooner. Not the homeless, mind, for they had tried to tell him for several years only to be executed en masse as a cost-cutting measure.

As the sun began to rise, William was reminded of his nights of excess. He stood up too quickly, stumbled, remembered the terrible cocaine hangovers he used to contend with after partying with landowners' associations. Eyes, limbs, soul all tired beyond compare, and yet his body twitched and pressed on as if controlled by a million ants burrowing into his flesh. He pressed on through the barren fields, walking hunched and slow like an Antarctic explorer, back when that was a possibility.

He came to a tall, dead tree at the top of a hill and stood beneath it. Looking at his surroundings, he could make out several ruined buildings nestled among the skeletal trees. The ground may as well have been salted, the sky a tapestry of greys, the whole world a thanatoid reminder of his sins. Their sins.

He slumped against the tree and succumbed to his exhaustion, dreaming briefly of his life in the city. Saw himself in the makeup chair at his television studio as a group of faceless drones applied his blush. *'What are you going to talk about?'* they wondered. What thing of little consequence was he going to pontificate upon that morning? Pronouns? Other people's dietary habits? The casting of a soon-to-be-forgotten film? 'No.' He looked into the mirror, his eyes were bleeding, his makeup made him look like a court jester. 'The end of the world.'

Stinging rain dropped on him as he rose from his nap, first as a gentle warning and then as a downpour. He leapt to his feet are ran down the hill, stumbling every now and then, but since it only made his descent faster, he was in no position to complain. Something had happened to the rain since the incident; it had become almost sulphuric in nature, killing what little man could not. William ran through blinding torrents until he came to a rusted car. Prying the door open, he sat inside and listened to the rhythmic thumping on the ceiling.

The car had belonged to a Mr and Mrs Jones. They never talked about politics as it was impolite. Months earlier they had been chased from their car and beaten to death. Their passivity couldn't save them. As for the car itself, William used his time to scour his surroundings for food or anything useful. Beneath the driver's seat he found a half-eaten chocolate bar, the brown outer shell now a mottled white, the nougat filling entwined with dirt and dust and tufts of hair. William ate it too quickly to notice. His gut bubbled and writhed, eyes bulged despite themselves, unused to the treat. At the manor, all the good food had been eaten within the first month, leaving in the end only beans, rice, and preserved halal jerky.

With fresh hope, William climbed into the backseat, exploring there and then the contents of the boot. He found only suitcases filled with money, jewellery, and clothes. Nothing he could use anymore. Returning to the passenger seat, he looked in the glovebox and saw only a map. A small village had been circled. His map reading skills were basic, but he could see the village was down the road and to the left. The Joneses had been so close. He rifled once more through the man's suitcase and took a jacket and a change of clothes. Then he sat and watched the rain hit the cracked glass as the memories of food began to vanish.

The rain did not stop until the following day. William looked out at the smoke rising from the ground. He was so hungry he could vomit. For the rest of the day he followed the map toward the village. Images of stocked pantries and warm beds abounded as he made his way down the road. His hopes and daydreams continued until he reached the crest of a small hill. This was where he first saw the village.

What he had hoped to find was not there. There was a village, to be sure, but it was far from empty. The perimeter had been cordoned with corrugated iron and barbed wire. The buildings were sandbagged and boarded up. Makeshift watchtowers surveyed the surrounding area. Wild dogs locked in cages began to howl as William drew closer. Alas, he didn't not notice the fascistic iconography unfurled on flagpoles until he, too, had been noticed by the residents.

'Come slowly to the gate,' a voice called out.

William obliged.

The gate was several layers of steel grating. William could see inside, see small groups of men running paramilitary drills outside the abandoned church, men in homemade SS uniforms march from one house to the next, shirtless men with shovels tilling what had been a cemetery. A boy's face appeared, blocking the view.

'What are you doing out here?' the boy asked.

'Just looking for shelter.'

'Right. You're white, yeah?'

William scoffed. 'I'm William Maypole, I'm sure even someone of your age can remember my shows.'

The boy scrunched his face. Boys of his disposition were incapable of not knowing something. 'Yeah, aye, yeah, I think so, yeah.'

'Won't you let me in, then? At least to clean up. Please, I've been walking for weeks.'

The boy nodded and reached for the gate's lock. A deep baritone yelled behind him. The boy turned. Marching toward the gate was a face William thought he would never see again.

'Jim!' he said, 'So great to see you.'

Jim, his former producer, didn't acknowledge him and instead looked at the boy. 'What are you doing?'

'This is William Daypo,' the boy explained, 'So I was letting him in.'

'This guy is a Muslim spy,' Jim corrected. 'He went to school in Dubai. Everyone knows this.'

The boy's hand snapped away from the gate's locks and his eyes were at once filled with contempt. 'Should I get the dogs?'

Jim looked at last at William. His face remained emotionless. 'No, as tainted as he is, he did some good work for us. Not enough. But some. Here's the deal, William, I'm letting you go this time, we won't even tell our superiors, but if we ever see you here again, I will personally feed you to the dogs. And they're as hungry as you are, so I'd be off if I were you.'

'But—' William tried to protest.

'I'd be off now if I were you.'

And with that William walked away. Years earlier, Jim would tell anyone who would listen that William was the only mentor worth having. Now, dogs snarled and chomped on metal bars while cruel men laughed at the marching dead.

As the evening once again drew near, William found himself in a forest. Surely, some part of him reasoned, there would be food in the forest. That there were still forests left at all was testament to natures durability. And, though the trees stood leafless and still, the ground beneath them showed signs of life. Succulent moss grew on stumps, mushrooms consumed the sides of hollowed trunks. Without thinking, William took a handful of the flat fungi and began the grind his teeth against their rough skin. He fought against all instincts and swallowed morsel after bitter morsel as he walked further into the woods. The terrain sloped downward, the air cold and still. For a moment he expected to hear birdsong. But there are no birds where there is no food. Even the carrion crow had departed long ago.

It was then he heard a woman's cry. He stopped, stood motionless, and listened again. It was the futile sobbing of a woman who had long since stopped believing in miracles.

He ran toward the sounds and came to a ravine. She lay at the bottom, her right leg broken and mangled by the fall. Her sobs stopped when she heard him, her head spun. William climbed down the embankment.

'Proszę, proszę,' she said as he drew close.

William looked at her. There she sat, haggard and old, her clothes several layers of black, eyes burnt shut by the rain, a growing pool of blood beneath her warped leg. Beside her was a backpack, the contents of which had spilled out onto the ground. Peanut butter, preserves, once the kind of thing a man of William's stature would turn his nose up at but now a veritable sack of treasures.

'Proszę. Muszę wrócić do mojego dziecka. Pomóż mi. Pomóż mi'

'I can't understand you.'

The woman's words were lost to wails as a fresh burst of pain shot through her. She struggled to point at her backpack, to some invisible point to behind William, to her own leg.

'You want me to talk the food?'

William began to stuff the jars back into the backpack, ignoring the woman next to him. The bag full, his appetite returned, he turned and began to walk away. The woman cried out behind him. Her words meant nothing to him, even the ones she screamed in English. She had been lucky, in a way, because foreign nationals should have been deported years earlier, and for her to still be walking England's virgin forests was further proof the people, not William, had failed.

The woman's cries became infrequent croaks and then nothing. William tried not to listen to her, instead following what he thought was the sounds of radio static. Instead, he pushed through the remains of the forest and came upon a small beach. The sun was low and his stomach empty. On the beach was an old hightide waiting station. It stood high above the ground atop four thick wooden legs. A small shack for shelter sat alone, almost floating. William walked toward it, climbing the broken steps to enter.

Inside, the shack had been ransacked. Old bloody palm prints painted the walls, the plexiglass windows cacked and scuffed. A lone stool lay undamaged amongst the wreckage, and William was quick to sit on it. He emptied the backpack on the floor before him and picked up a jar of peanut butter. He ate. He ate for all the meals he had missed, for all the future meals he would not have. His stomach tried to rebel against him, unused to so much so quickly, but William forced the contents of each and every jar before him down his throat until he sat, out of breath, bloated, tired, facing out toward the sea. Then he slept as best he could, the wind and waves outside slamming against the walls outside, his insides struggling to digest his feast.

In the morning he thought he heard seagulls. The room was cold and his limbs stiff. Everything creaked in unison as he stood. Outside looked clear and he thought, for a moment, the last year of his life had been one tremendous nightmare. His appetite sated, tiredness gone, he felt as he had some time ago. With a newfound energy, he changed into Jones' clothes and stepped outside.

Unfortunately, William did not look down, and was too confident in his step. The ageing wood of the shack broke beneath his feet and he plummeted into the high tide. The current was strong, it tugged on him like the half-forgotten refugees had. Pulling him out to sea, he was too full, too shocked, to fight back. He tried to float as best he could as the waves tossed him around. After what felt like an old-fashioned drubbing, his consciousness waned, and for a moment he welcomed death.

But death was not ready for him yet.

He woke once more on the coast. A lone gull called out again. Where there were once organs inside him, it felt as if he had been hollowed out, skin replaced by polished brash, and then struck with a drumstick. His arms flailed of their own accord, legs unwilling to put in even the minimum amount of work required to move, eyes opened and closed without permission. For a while, he thought he could hear himself snore. The side of his forehead stung with each fresh lick of the water. When his eyes were open the light in the sky would become a kaleidoscope of blurs. If he was going to die, he hoped his lucidity would fail him first.

A lifting motion. He was floating. No, he actually was floating. Leather and canvas strained beneath him and two gruff sets of lungs let out small sighs as he hovered off the beach. Footsteps in the sand, more than two people walking. William became aware of a presence to his right. He titled his head, a bearded man walked by his side staring forward with dispassionate blankness until he noticed William's eyes upon him. Then a smile.

'Ah, so you can move. We've been trying to talk to you for half an hour.'

'Wha-uh, what?' William struggled to speak.

'Rest up, lad, we have a bit of a walk ahead of us. Lucky we came by you when we did, man, it'd be a week or more before our next patrol, and there's no telling what would have happened in that time.' The man shuddered slightly, suggesting he knew exactly what fate would have found William.

They walked in near silence for an hour or so, William's strength slowly returning. He could wiggle his toes, command his hands, even look up without spectral auras appearing. He was going to live. For how long he did not know. At the very least, he did not get the impression his rescuers were cannibals, and he had yet to be fed to dogs.

All at once, the sounds of life filled William's ears. People yelled greetings at the bearded man, who returned in kind. Animals made noises at no one in particular, wooden wheels and mill systems spun, water trickled into cobbled-together filtration systems.

Children played with old footballs and older people sat on rocking chairs outside their shacks, huts, and tents. Everyone was smiling. Back at the manor, nobody had smiled even before the end began.

William was shocked. Shocked by a working farm, by so many people living in harmony, by the complete lack of wanky bum-bum. More than that, though, he was shocked to see a woman in a hijab walking arm in arm with a redheaded man in a kilt. The bearded saviour saw William's confusion.

'Oh, I know, right? Weird couple, what with her being a Taurus and him being a Pisces. But this place has really brought us all together. And you know what? In a silver-lining kind of way, we're all happier for it.'

Their solidarity did save them.

'When you're ready and able, if you want to stay, you're going to need to pull your weight. We're all in this together. That fine with you?'

'…Yeah.'

The lowered the stretcher by an empty shack. The two carriers left William and the bearded man. There was still much to process. Finally, after several garbled attempts, William was able to speak a full sentence. He looked his saviour in the eyes and tried to smile.

'Thank you. Thank you for saving me. I owe you my life.'

'You'd do the same for me, right?'

William looked up, eyes furrowed, as if he didn't understand.

'I said, you'd do the same for me, right?'

He couldn't answer that.

Remnants of a Lost Novel

Iteration 1a

And all at once, I am in Iceland, the immigration booths looming ahead of me, the point of no return. The past twenty years of my life already a jumbled blur behind me. My mind uncoils, trying to think of the right answers to the imminent checkpoint interrogation. Who am I? Where am I going? Where am I coming from? Do I mind coming this way for further questions? Try as I might, I've never been able to answer any of these succinctly enough to please an immigration officer.

"Welcome, enjoy your stay."

I stare at the attendant for a second, unsure if they're talking to me. They are. The next visitor nudges me to one side and I'm through without even knowing it.

The airport is familiar, it feels like a regular childhood trip to a warehouse furniture store. Like the furniture store, most of the people around me are too busy trying to find their own chair to care about someone else's. Most people don't care about anything beyond their own immediate needs.

As I pass through the cavernous metallic arrival section, I try to visualise a map of the area I'd tried to download. My phone, two months behind on bills, is not cooperating. Understandably. There is supposed to be a cycle path out in the parking facility somewhere, leading off toward my destination. No more taxis for me, no more buses. No more money. Besides which, I ratio- nalise, a walk through an alien wilderness is not an opportunity I get often.

Outside, I am greeted by a wet gust of nothing. What was supposed (in my mind) a large parking structure, is actually a patchwork quilt of lots, separated by lines of earth. Beyond those, a mossy field of drab browns and greens, but that is as far as I can see, as the far distance is concealed by a thick soup of swirling mist. It's as if I have been encases in the centre of a glass dome: as I move, so does my field of vision, like a giant invisible thumb is sliding the dome forward with me.

After walking through a trio of empty lots, I find what I presume to be the cycle path. Except it's not so much a path as it is a thick, black sludge, poured haphazardly over the volcanic rocks underneath in some gross approximation of a straight line. I follow it, uncomfortably aware of its proximity to the airport's wire fencing and the accompanying knowledge that in some countries I'd at the very least have a sniper trained on me from a watchtower. In the distance, through the mist, I can make out glimpses of jagged cliffs, the ocean, viable hiking terrain, but these promises of a world worth exploring are short lived and all too quickly disappear from my sight.

Nothing seemed to change while I walked, if anything, it felt like my surroundings were becoming pared down. All I had for company for some time was the slug trail of tar beneath me and the autumnal ground to either side. And the fog, the impenetrable fog. There was nothing to indicate that I was even walking the right way, but I had no real option other than to press on. Then, behind me, a cough.

I turned casually to see who was walking with me, hoping they could reassure my navigational ability. No no. No one anywhere. I stood still and tried to listen for another cough, or some sign of life. Nothing. Then, as I stared at the wall of dense smoke I could see a figure slowly form just behind it. The figure slowly moved toward me and then--

The unexpected whoosh of a passing truck rattled in my ear and I turned abruptly to see the road was a lot closer to me than I had expected. Several cars drove by in quick succession, coming out of nowhere, all heading toward the airport. I pushed forward, trying to ignore the stranger behind me. It was probably for the best - who wants to get so wrapped up in pointless paranoia that they're killed by oncoming traffic?

As I continued to walk, it began to seem like the vehicles were driving in a set sequence. Brown truck, white car, grey van, yellow bus, silver car, again and again, just frequent enough to keep me focused on not getting annihilated. Although the cycle path had faded into little more than a lay-by, everything else remained unchanging, even the steady flow of traffic becoming part of the constant. Eager to get indoors, I looked down at my watch. The directions had suggested the walk would only take thirty or so minutes, according to my watch, however, I'd been walking for three hours.

All this to save a few krona.

I stopped. To my left, a small town, more a random spattering of white buildings, revealed itself under the misty blanket. From a distance, it looked tranquil, but then so do most things. Even a corpse looks peaceful if you see it from the right angle. It was easy to imagine the little community as a peaceful gathering of fishermen, maybe a few isolated artists, a place where people could retreat when things got too difficult. And by "things" I mean the unrelenting and indifferent master of us all. As nice as the brief exercise in make believe was, the town probably had its own dark secrets bubbling up just underneath the surface.

It was only when I began to walk again that my legs started to feel stiff. My pants had soaked through so slowly that I hadn't noticed. All at once I was eager to get to my destination. To warm up. To undress in an appropriate setting. I stopped again to check my backpack - my damp pants were one thing, but a ruined book was something else entirely.

Beyond the town, the mist had dispersed, and I could look out onto the sharkskin ocean, the ragged cliffs, the sloping hills. Elsewhere, I could see that the airport was still nearby, wide open, unchanging plains went off in all directions. Strangers were walking dogs, riding bike, both. Faint rainbows peppered the atmosphere like the memory of a pride parade. Behind me, the crunching of gravel, a cough, someone reaching out to me.

A small, blue car pulled into the gravel just ahead of me. The car was all right angles, like east bloc architecture. I approached the passenger side of the vehicle and communicated with the driver using international hand gestures. The driver casually waving me inside, me mock-flattered, politely trying to turn them down just enough so that they wouldn't drive away. After the two prerequisite refusals to get in the vehicle, I got in the vehicle. It's a learned trained - only accepting something the third time it's offered - and one with fairly obvious risks. Sometimes you're only offered something once.

But, anyway, after the well-rehearsed dance of my people was behind us I tried to cram myself into the passenger seat. The tiny interior forced my joints into unnatural positions, knees pressed up against the golden statue on the dashboard. The driver, as large as they were, must have been born and raised inside the vehicle. That's the only way they could appear so comfortable.

Once I was as close a proximity to sitting down as I was going to get, the driver put the car in gear. "Where are you from?" they asked.

"Originally? England."

"Oh, of course." They smiled as if they understood everything already. The car slowly moved toward a roundabout. "Ah!" the driver gasped.

My seatbelt. I had forgotten to put on my seatbelt, for the first time in years. The driver gaped in abject horror for the three seconds it took me to correct this mistake.

Continuing forward, the driver coughed. "So what are you doing here?"

"I'm starting to wonder that myself."

"No, but, I mean do you have something planned?"

"Home. I'm going home."

Nodding, the driver looked at me, "Sounds like you're not sure about that."

"It's a long story, look--"

"We're here."

The hostel was already in front of us as the miniature car parked. A converted air force barrack, painted in red and blue camouflage, colours as impractical for camouflage as they are visually pleasing. Massive antique spotlights had been pointed toward the hostel's walls, illuminating the paint and the hostel's name even in daylight.

"Good luck on your journey."

"Same to you."

Beneath its thin beige veneer, the Hostel told ghost stories. Behind the slapdash paint job and new, midrange furnishings were the old scars of a military station. Deactivated sirens hidden behind pot plants, designations and old billboards protruded slightly through the paint, detailing old intrusions and phone extensions that led to nowhere. Tiny metal phone booths jutted out of corners, once a source of connection to those stationed there, now only impractical furniture, found art. The dozens of bookshelves have been littered with just as many old gas-masks and hats as they have guide books. And then there is the implacable snoring. As I wait for check in to open, a metronomic snoring reverberates through the thick walls, the disused pipes, in such a way that it was as if I was inside a sleeping giant. Despite trying to find some sleeping backpacker, I found no one, and the snore maintained a constant volume.

Which at least meant the beds were probably comfortable.

The reception area took up most of the ground floor and also served as a gift shop which also served as a taxi service which also served as a kitchen. It was surrounded by high walls, so all you good see was the blue glow of computer screens and the top of someone's bobbing head. They were nodding rhythmically to some timeless European electronica which made it difficult to get their attention. Once I did, though, it took all of three seconds to get the key card and room number.

Isn't that usually how it goes?

The dorms were in a separate set of barracks, an empty, gutted building with never-ending corridors. Once again, snoring seemed to echo through the walls, though less synchronised than they had been. It was as if the entire building had apnoea. Walking like a trespasser, I slowly made my way to the fifth floor, the home of my dorm. A naive part of me was excited to check out the views from the window. My thoughts were interrupted when I began climbing the stairs and my hand touched something wet and stiff, like a skinned deer. The banisters and railings of the stairwell had been covered in damp clothes of varying sizes and colours. The windowsills, iron radiators, even old filing cabinets too cumbersome to remove were coated with a layer of neatly folded garments. At the top floor, finally, I could see into the communal dining room, devoid of people but containing various nests of unwashed bowls, a trio of small, round tables coated with the remnants of someone's breakfast. The snoring grew louder as I tried to find my room.

As I reached the door of my dorm, I could hear a telephone - that old-fashioned ringing you seldom hear any more - ringing from the end of the hall. It wasn't for me.

The dorm was comprised of six bunk beds and very little room for movement. The room had the dimensions of someone's office, an officer's office, which didn't exactly lend itself to what you want for a twelve-person dorm. There was a single cabinet, a single plug socket, and as much as I hoped I had the room to myself, part of me wanted to watch more territorial travellers vie for control over the limited resources. My feet grew a size as I struggled to remove my shoes for the first time in two days. I just needed a quick lie down. Only for a minute. Only for a minute. I had museums to visits.

*

There's nothing quite like the experience of nodding off alone in a room only to wake up in a place full of busy strangers. At first it's surprising, an invasion of space, unexpected guests seeing you at your most vulnerable, but once you regain your faculties and realize you're in the same place you were, it's oddly comforting - you are, after all, unmolested and safe. It serves as a brief reminder that if most people aren't inherently good, they are at least grossly indifferent. And so, it was that evening when I came to, fully clothed and groggy, with three groups of significantly different strangers congregating in the other three corners of the room, engaged in conversations in three languages I couldn't quite place.

Silently, I stuffed my sore feet into my boots and limped outside.

The hostel was connected to a network of abandoned, identical buildings, all shuttered up and barricaded which seemed to serve the opposite of purpose. At the very least the buildings could be shelter, but they were denied even that possibility. Worse than the empty buildings, though, were the unused parks. A swing with no one to enjoy it made me think of the distant future.

I turned around and walked toward lights and life.

The museum was closing as I neared it, lights already off inside, the younger employees waving at their apparent supervisor as they ran toward waiting cars.

I'm alone again in another empty dorm, this one not too far from the city's main railway station. The racket of a never-ending laundry cycle beats through the wall beside my bunk. Outside, the duet of morning traffic and departing trains proves relaxing. So much of my past is already resigned to the hazy labyrinth of memory. Where was I last week? *Remind me.* What was I doing at this precise moment a month ago? If felt useless to cling to fragmented facts that no longer seemed important, much less the ones I had to strain to visualise.

At the very least, I could actually see the other guests sulking around the hostel. An improvement. They were young, lugubrious travellers, more concerned with sticking to a strict itinerary written by an anonymous travel guru than actually seeing the city for themselves.

Yearning for conversation - it had been a while - I tried to talk to a few of them in the common area but struggled to get beyond basic platitudes. 'Hey,' I'd say. 'Oh, hi,' their reply. 'Got any plans for today?' 'Uh, no, no real plans, no.' And so on. It was like having the sudden impulse to paint only to find that the one colour left on the palette was a drab grey.

My chances for involved conversation diminished in the dining area. Several groups had congregated around massive tables, enjoying their bread-based *free* breakfasts. I try to sit in vacant seats, only for those around me to shuffle together, close ranks. For self-proclaimed world citizens, hungry for adventure, it was surprising they were only capable of talking to their own kind. I didn't have the right aura. When had I become so unapproachable?

It became apparent that if I wanted someone to actually talk to, I'd have to go elsewhere. So, I did. Stuffing four miniature croissants into my maw, I walked out onto the busy street.

Before I could even take in a breath of fresh air, I found myself engulfed by a flowing current. People who had no idea where they were going but were frantic to get there pulled me down the street. Tourists, in particular, had always left me feeling like I didn't exist. I could relate to the huddled figures who clung to the edges of peripheral vision. The hidden shadow people sitting under doorways or pressed up underneath ATMs. The hunched sleeping bags chatting to themselves on bridges while the world marched on.

What made *me* feel invisible was: you could be walking down any of the more popular streets, and, within a few seconds, someone in front of you would stop without warning. They just had to take some uninspired photo, and your body would jerk to a halt. To the milling masses, you either didn't exist or you were something in the way. Walking up the road was an obstacle course full of whirling umbrellas, ankle-bashing scooters, and flailing limbs. Each step forward saw a new threat, each small slight a wound to my existential self-worth. Didn't I deserve to feel like I existed?

The only people who did seem to acknowledge those around them were looking to make some easy money. Or, worse yet, desperate artists searching for photogenic homeless people.

Swathes of intercontinental groups clogged alleyways, passages, entrances, rendering some of the most popular destinations borderline inaccessible. And yet, despite all this, there wasn't much to say. Only: 'No, sorry, I don't have any money.' 'Hey, watch out, you almost hit me.' 'I'm not interested in your new religion, but thank you, no, thank you, I've got to go, though, no, sorry, I don't need a free test, sorry.' Not exactly life-changing conversations.

It was obvious I wasn't going to have a real conversation with anyone on the busy streets, so I did the logical thing and entered a nearby graveyard. It wouldn't take much for the dead to be more talkative. Decades of industrial progress had blackened the stone walls. Acid rain and age had claimed the names and details of even the most important residents. Huge, ornate monuments complete with sculptures of skeletons and angels were transforming into little more than meaningless mounds of warped stone. The bodies below weren't the only things fading away into nothing.

In the corners of the cemetery, in full view of everyone, people had set up small campsites. Sitting around makeshift barbecues, the campers were having hushed conversations, ignorant of where they were. Elsewhere, small groups of uninterested visitors walked among the burial grounds.

I walked with some trepidation toward the nearest set of tents. Three people about my age huddled together, sharing a large can of lager. Would they want to talk? As I drew closer, a strange sense of defensiveness began to unfurl. They eyeballed me with suspicion as I got closer. Could they know? Did they know?

Retreating to the middle of the grounds, I wondered if anyone else knew they were in a cemetery. Aside from the campers in the corners, there were people having romantic picnics on tombs. Impatient lovers leaned against worn gravestones with their full weight while they waited on their partner. The general contempt for the dead was palpable. It felt less like strangers paying their respects on hallowed lands, more an awkward family reunion at some community building where they'd already lost the deposit.

My attention turned to a roving gang of wizards who had entered through one of the many iron gates. Wizards? Definitely not something I expected to see in a decaying burial ground. As the wizards got closer, I could see that many of them were children, cloaked preteens armed with plastic brooms and sticks. I had always assumed that wizards were older and antisocial. Seeing so many in one place dispelled several of my preconceived ideas.

I could hear the young sorcerers laugh as they walked by. They were being led through the area by a dead-eyed PHD candidate - you can always spot a PHD candidate by their ability to both look youthful and ancient at the same time. It looked like some of the monuments were of particular interest to the wandering magicians. I watched with an unexpected sense of longing as they disappeared around a corner.   My disappointment was short lived as two more groups of similar wizards materialised through the same iron gates. Each group followed their own desiccated intellectual. Lingering in the entryway of a ransacked mausoleum, I waited for the second group to pass and marched to their rear. I was close enough to their conversations to pretend I was taking part. Grinning and nodding along while their leader winded between the graves, I felt like part of the group. Nobody seemed to mind that I was there. I did not understand any of the titbits the head wizard kept bringing up but tried to play along. The rest of our group gasped at regular intervals. I had no idea I was in such an important landmark.

Finally, we reached our destination. I knew it was the end because the ageless head wizard said 'OK, everyone, this is the end!' We'd stopped at a small plaque on a grey wall, fenced off from the surrounding plaques and graves. The group stared in silence, their collective mouths agape. Some took happy group photos and left small notes or flowers. Others kissed the deceased's engraved name with a reverence reserved for royalty and genitalia.

At least one wizard bawled for several minutes. One by one, the group of wizards dispersed, misty-eyed but fulfilled. I was alone again, staring at something I didn't understand.

Whose plaque was it?

Dale D Mortish.
No idea.'

As I was exiting the cemetery, put off by the growing number of pilgrimaging wizards, I noticed that, not too far from the city, there was an imposing hill. If nothing else, it was a welcomed chance to get away from the maddening crowds of wizards and neophyte photographers. While hills have never been particularly well-known for their conversations, I assumed that anyone up there would be more inclined to talk to me. Or that was the plan, at least. Plus, too, even if I found no one up there, I'd still be alone on the top of a hill. It was a non-zero-sum game.

At that point, though, I would have made do with a quick chat. A simple 'Can you take my photo?' 'Oh, yeah, sure, no problem at all!' 'Great! Thank you so much!' 'Don't mention it, mate.' 'Did you want one? A photo I mean?' 'What? Oh, no, no, I'm good, wanted to feel dizzy for a minute.' Something like that. I wasn't hoping for that exact conversation occur, because who would hope for a conversation like that? I'd have been happy with anything, anything to break the vow of silence loneliness had placed upon me.

The path at the base of the hill branched off in several directions. I paused, trying to decide which one would be most popular with like-minded individuals. The information board, in a shocking turn of events, didn't offer that kind of information.

I didn't notice them while I was looking at the map, but someone had been sitting beside the placard. As I traced the possible routes, they lurched forward unannounced. They were wearing the reflective vest of a construction worker and the shoes of a vagrant.

'All these paths branch off again, and then those paths branch off again, too. But whichever way you walk, you end up at the same place,' they said.

'At the… at the top?' I offered, in the non-committal tone of someone who wasn't sure if they'd answered a rhetorical question.

'No, back down at the bottom,' they smiled. 'But there was a landslide thataway, so I'd pick another path.'

'Is the top worth the walk?'

'What is?'

With my conversation quotient for the week fulfilled, I made my way up the hill with a smile. The smile faded as I began to realise both how long the walk was going to take and how unhealthy I'd become. But my poor exercise habits were easy to ignore with so many views to admire. The city was larger than any of the tourists below would ever know. It was an expansive patchwork quilt of historical buildings, parks, and vestiges of centuries past. To the east, my friend the ocean, as angry as ever. Small fingers of land pointed outward like they were trying to reach for something. In all other directions, was the promise of future hikes, an ageless, green expanse that disappeared beyond the horizon.

Toward the summit, the pathways faded into nothing more than jagged stones. There was no clear way to the crown of stones that anointed the top of the hill. With no marked route, I had to think about each step. One wrong choice and I would find myself at the receiving end of an immobilising attack of vertigo, or worse. Looking down for the more worn sections of rock, and spotting a helpful trail of crushed beer cans, I made my final march to the peak. There was no one else there. Whatever brief interview I'd imagined had eluded me.

I closed my eyes, took a deep breath, and prepared to survey the majestic vistas beneath me. When I opened my eyes, the ground had vanished. The city, the ocean, the rolling hills, all gone. Replaced with nothing.

Imagine this:

Except forever. All that seemed to exist at that moment was me and a chaotic assortment of floating rocks.

'Can you take my photo?' said a familiar voice behind me.

♩♩♩

That night, I was walking around the outer edge of the tourism hub, trying to forget that little mental slip on the hill. I had been eating at random intervals, so if anything, it was a wonder it had taken so long for my old issues with syncope to return. Days of surviving on nothing but cheap energy bars and bitter hostel coffee will do that to you. It was my bodies way of telling me to eat real food.

The street I happened to be on was a long row of imposing Victorian houses. They had long since become dental practises, various offices, upscale psychics. Far too expensive for anyone to actually live in them. As I walked down the empty street, I couldn't help but look through the windows, hoping to see some glimpse of real life.   Nothing.

It was only when I reached the end of the street that something stood out. A small arrow made up of flashing LEDs beckoned me to follow down a small staircase. Climbing down, I found myself beneath an ophthalmologist's office. A thick black door stood open, the entrance to some dingy room. Peeking through the doorway, I could see that inside was a comedy club and since I needed a laugh I entered.

Guarding the entrance was that same greasy haired, unimposing, black-clad bouncer who seemed to work in every bar and nightclub I'd ever been in. Their posture overcompensated for their lack of stature, and a perpetual scowl rested above their sunken, dull eyes. They were friendly enough.

A small bar took up the wall closest to me. It was smaller than what seemed reasonable, six foot long. Even with me as the only customer, the two bartenders would have to jostle for position to fulfil even the simplest of orders.

When I entered, I thought I was in a modest little space, but as I walked to the seats, I saw that it was a large, L-shaped room. The longer part of the L took up the back wall, in the middle of which was a low, elevated stage, roughly the size of a small bathroom. A slapdash collection of chairs surrounded the stage, all but empty.

The interior was a matt black, but closer to the bar were a few stapled neon flyers. On the back wall, there was a vivid mural of a teenaged boy getting his brains blown out. A thick, haggard hand squeezed down on the trigger of an antique Luger. A bullet had already torn through the opposite side of the head, with blood, brain, and pia mater erupting across the entire length of the wall. Each nugget of gore had become an anthropomorphic face as if they had been repurposed for a children's film. Each little terror show of human detritus gave their jovial thumbs up to no one in particular.

While I was confident that the comedians would opt to tell actual jokes there was a chance they'd engage in audience participation. To be safe I sat stage left, nestled behind a pillar. The chances of a plucky comedian finding and embarrassing me from the safety of their stage were slim.

Sitting there bored with nothing to do and less to look at, I took out the scrap of paper the bouncer had given me. The show, an "experimental open mic assortment of shite," wouldn't start for another hour. I leaned back in my seat and watched as other people entered and became the audience. Most of them fit into three categories: tepid dates with at least one ashamed party; nervous groups of bland office drones who had wrapped up that day's uninspiring workshop; drunken locals. I let out a small sigh of relief each time someone sat down. The comedians had enough material.

The lights cut out without warning, and the familiar opening bars of an old pop song blared out, silencing the chuntering audience. A diminutive comedian stepped onto the stage to a smattering of applause. She grasped the microphone like a lost limb.

'Aw, hello, out there!' she screamed into the microphone. 'Big crowd for a Wednesday, no?'

She paced around like a zooed predator. 'Well, it's a Wednesday show, like I say, so that means we give nae fucks tonight. If it's your first time here, don't get too nervous! If it's not your first time, I THOUGHT WE TOLD YOU NEVER TO COME BACK! I'm joking, I'm joking. Hey, so, anyone from out of town out there tonight?'

And so, began the emcee's set. Her shtick was that she'd ask the audience questions and then ridicule anyone who was nice enough to answer. That was it, the entirety of her routine. She resonated most with a pair of drunks sitting at the very front, which seemed like a tactical error on the comedian's part. She wanted to engage as many people as possible, but the drunks would continue to interject, struggling to shift the focus back onto them.

When the emcee was content with the number of paying customers she had lambasted, she introduced another comedian. The second act bumbled through two jokes about living alone before co-opting the emcee's patter. The third act was more of the same, as was the fourth, the fifth. It was becoming less a comedy show and more an act of public flagellation. As I sat through the barrage of insults, the strangers in the audience became human. They would reveal a little too much when pressed by the comedians.

'I hate my job. All I'm doing with my life is ushering in the apocalypse so my shitty boss can get a bonus,' said one of the conference people.

'This is our third date and since neither of us has a discernible personality, we thought we'd come here and laugh. Then we're going to go home and have unfulfilling sex,' said one of the doomed couples, in unison.

'Every day my soul screams out in pain. Every day those screams are for nothing. I have become a walking death rattle,' a voice called out from the darkness.

The comedians became less and less interested in delivering actual jokes. Each question became more personal than the last, each answer more candid. People were pushing their chairs forward, trying to get closer to the stage, eager to auction off their personal traumas. I sat transfixed, worried about what they'd ask me.

The few lights illuminating the room dimmed into nothingness. Soon, all that remained was a single beam emitting upwards from the stage. A slow, plodding version of the show's intro music played. If it wasn't for the pillar I was leaning against, I would have felt ephemeral, a phantom floating toward a black hole.

The emcee from earlier stepped into the light. Not even her drunk friends from earlier applauded. Her smile had vanished, her energy sapped. 'Our last comedian tonight,' she said, flicking a limp wrist to her left. Then, without uttering another sound, she stepped forward out of the light and vanished.

An almost-human figure emerged from the darkness and floated into the beam. All I could see was a tight crimson jacket and a crisp, white shirt. The figure levitated for a second. I could sense that somewhere in the darkness its eyes were looking out into the crowd, searching. The torso leaned forward toward the microphone.

'Oh, hello there, what a big crowd for a Thursday,' a booming voice said. 'I can see you out there, alone in the black. Don't think I don't see you. I know what you've done. Who you are. Any sinners in the audience tonight?'

Without thinking, I raised my hand. The pillar I was leaning against seemed to float away and evaporate.

'No need for you to say what you've done. We know. We all know. Everyone knows.'

I searched the audience, trying to find the dull glimmer of accusatory eyes staring back at me, but there was nothing there. I stood to object, to justify my choices, to defend my past to an invisible, judgemental audience, but the only sound that came out of my mouth was laughter.

'Do you seek forgiveness?'

Laughter again. Mine, but not from me.

'Do you want to confess?'

The laughter took its own form and bounced away from me through the darkness, its echoes mocking me, compelling me to follow. My legs wouldn't let me. My legs were gone. I had gone. The only thing that was real was the crimson jacket on the stage, its arms reaching out for me.

'Soon.'

Applause. Grateful whistles. Hoots and hollers. The torso bows deeply and fades away. The house lights snapped back on, and all at once

<u>Iteration 2</u>

I wake up on a stiff red and white seat, my face pressed against a cold plastic window, crystallized drool smeared on the surface against my cheek. Next to me, in an identical seat, a cadaverous stranger is sleeping. Across from us, two more strangers hang their heads as they snooze against each other. The many rows of unconscious travellers are in a sterile carriage hurtling down a shoreline. The train rocked like a heavy cradle as it raced to its destination. It's early in the morning, an egg yolk sun creeps ever upward above a placid 0093AF sea; the sky a tableau of pinks, oranges, and greys. Above, the accumulating virga promise a damp evening. Outside, I could see the history of the land play out in front of me, the prehistoric scars of shifting glaciers, volcanoes, tectonic shifts. It was a past full of sulphur, smoke, ice, and rain - much like the city itself as one of the comedians said from... from? I couldn't remember.

I leaned back. The train was too full, and the air tasted like bleached vomit, something I recognised from earlier years. The comatose passengers around me were in stasis, not a snore nor a shuffle nor a cough seeped out. Finally. As much as I tried to fall back to sleep, I couldn't find the energy to close my eyes. Instead, I looked off into the warped reflection of the sun and dreamt of dreaming.

♪♪♪

It seems that whenever I plan on travelling, sooner or later it turns out that I've completely overlooked a national holiday. Showing up to a tropical city unprepared for Carnival, trying to get work done on a bank holiday, the usual. It was the same perplexing experience when the train finally pulled into my station. Something big must have been happening, but I had no idea what. From every direction, I could see the inordinate number of passengers arriving. The herd corralled itself into too few automated ticket machines as we rushed for the exits.

Waiting beyond the ticket machines were huge crowds of well-dressed people. They were milling around, searching for people, trains, food. Soon, I found myself wedged between two groups of businessmen. I struggled to reach down for my ticket because my arms had become interlinked with others trying to do the same. The thick smoke of locomotives hung low, and the sounds of too many steam whistles echoed all around me. The station was a bustling microcosm of self-preservation, far more chaotic than the last time I was there.

We should do that ag- No.

I pushed against a tide of people wearing their Sunday best and tried to block out the sight of the urchins who hid in the darkened edges of the station. It was hard to ignore them, though - in a flowing river, it's the stationary rocks that stand out. Train terminals were where you got to see people at their most unfiltered, free from the performative version of their lives. If you ever want to see someone's true self, take them to a busy place and tell them they're late. They'll be more than happy to show you who they are.

Most of them you'd come to see as dangerous mercenaries.

Much like the priest in front of me who didn't think anyone noticed when they shoulder barged a pensioner to get to an empty seat, I could try to pretend there wasn't some unpleasant side to me. But it was there, deep down, in some dark, cavernous recess of my mind. Self-reproach combined with the stench of burnt fuels, the pull of nagging crowds, and the floating echoes of perpetual action made me feel uneasy. Everything seemed to press down on me, crushing me. I couldn't breathe. I pushed by the pensioner, still recovering from the priest's attack, and ran outside.

Wasn't I supposed to wait for someone?

Outside was unfamiliar, not the town I'd left many years before. The buildings were sooty and oppressive. The road's tarmac was gone, exposing the packed soil underneath. The neighs of an approaching horse-drawn

'Hey!'

I turned.

My mother. Almost definitely my mother. Same stature, same chipper voice, same hopeful mannerisms. I had to focus to ensure it was her. 'Hiya!' A hug, a peck on the cheek. 'You walked right past me!' her voice at once happy and betraying a polite agitation I knew all too well. It was definitely her.

Prosopagnosia. That's the simple truth of the matter. I have never recognised a face, and never will. This ruined any hopes of working in a detective agency or as a portrait artist, but it did force me to look at people a lot harder than most. And that's the last time I'll explain something to you.

'Hey, mam,' I said, giving a hug of my own.

'Sorry I'm late. Were you worried? You seemed worried when you ran by.'

'No, my train got here a minute ago.'

She paused, took a moment to acknowledge I was standing right next to her. 'Where's all your stuff?'

My thumb pointed at my backpack.

'Is that it?'

'Yeah, I didn't have time to pack anything else.'

Which was true, even if it was also true that I didn't have much to pack. The decision to return home had been impromptu, an event I'll never comprehend. *If you'd only* - Not now.

'We'll take you shopping, then.'

'Not today. I'm shattered.'

We walked away from the station, passing roads jammed by an eclectic mix of cars. There was almost nobody on the sidewalks. A few small groups of people broke through the white noise of city life with their loud, jocular conversations.

The drive brought to light mum's journey toward self-discovery. She'd bought a rowboat, a violin, taken up MMA and pottery, lessons in Japanese speaking and French cooking. It was great to see her excited to talk about so many new paths in her life, not least because it meant I didn't have to talk about myself.

It's interesting to see how much a place changes over time. To see what survives and what dies. Which soulless conglomerate replaces which cherished childhood spot. Which direction gentrification decided to flow. It was depressing to see how little the motorway had changed. But as we drove the buildings warped, at odds with my own memories. Wasn't that a field? Didn't those affordable condominiums use to be a family cinema or a museum or a fire station or something? When did the dodgy street, famous for knife violence, become a row of upmarket coffee shops? As we got close to the coast, the buildings disappeared, replaced by clods of soil and crumbling stone. Entire streets demolished by optimistic property developers, then abandoned when they ran out of money. All that remained standing was a single cream cottage on the corner of a once-busy street.

We pulled into the driveway; an act that struck me as redundant. The cottage's yard was a vibrant green made all the greener thanks to the surrounding vacant lots. I followed my mother up a small path to the front door and turned to see an unobstructed view of the North Sea.

'Well, these are your digs for now. I know it's a bit of a war zone right now, but it's taking forever to sort out the guest room.'

'It's perfect. I could stay here for a while.'

'They're knocking it down in two months, so don't get too attached.'

Inside was almost barren. A sagging cast-off futon the sole object in the living room. The remains of a plastic picnic set had been set up in the dining space. A lone towel, not much larger than a tissue, hung over the rusted railings of a shower stall. A giant air mattress took up most of the bedroom. In the kitchen, someone had been nice enough to leave behind a small stack of books to make up for the lack of television. Even without the books, it was everything I always pretended to want - an opportunity to live a pared down lifestyle. Simplicity. A chance to focus on old projects without the usual distractions.

I had explored the house twice before noticing that my mother had been talking the entire time. Nodding, I hoped my vague affirmations would be enough to convince her I'd been listening.

'You would love it over there,' she said.

'Where?'

'Vietnam! I told you.'

'Who is going to Vietnam?'

'I am! Tomorrow evening, sweety. You're jetlagged.'

'So, the guest room?'

'When I get back! You've got this whole house!'

'Oh, no, no, I didn't mean to sound like an ingrate. I've slept in way worse places than this, I thought...' *Cold, unforgiving concrete slabs hidden behind thick, metal doors. Rain-soaked park benches. Hospital waiting rooms. Padded rubber cots with rounded corners in an empty room with glass walls. A sleeping bag tucked behind the decaying hay of an abandoned farm.* 'I thought we'd see each other more.'

The front door swung open before she could answer. A paw of a hand grasped the wooden frame of the doorway and propelled a giant man into existence. He was wearing a burgundy suit jacket, distressed jeans, and a bushy beard. He looked like the youthful host of a mid-afternoon game show, or the hip CEO of an exploitative tech company. He walked across the room like he was on television - self-aware, confident, walking toward his pre-rehearsed markers. I didn't recognise him, but my mother was quick to her feet, wrapping her arms around him. They both seemed very happy; mum changed her demeanour in an instant. A new boyfriend? Neighbour? But there are no neighbours? So, someone from church or a Buddhist retreat or pottery or or or?

'Aren't you going to give your brother a hug?'

The man lumbered over, picking me up without much effort for a tight embrace. 'Welcome home! It's been too long!'

He was right, it had been too long. An eternity in fact.

I don't have a brother.

You sit on an antique leather bench - comfortable for its age - facing three plastic chairs. Each chair seats a jittery person who could be mistaken for you if you caught a fleeting glimpse of them. A passing drunk would insist that they were you. Turning away from the doppelgangers, you try to look at your surroundings. Where are you? The walls look like the remnants of a tart Shiraz left to encrust the seabed of a giant glass. The floor is a cigar-smoke swirl of marble that runs off into nothingness. Honey hues illuminate the hall, but you can't find a source for the lights. They're emanating from nothing. A click-clack of authoritative heels approach and you are all at once dwarfed by a tall, slender figure that looms over the entire hallway. Their face is hidden in the shadows of their own creation. Their Hyperborean arms wrap around a metal clipboard. Then, their long, skeletal index finger runs down their list, searching for something. Ah! They find it.

'We're ready for your audition now.'

You're escorted onto a stage and stand on an island of mahogany. In every direction, there is only darkness. All you can see is the floor beneath you and an impenetrable light above. You turn once, twice, too many times, until you can no longer ascertain if you're facing the audience or the back wall.

A voice roars out from all directions. 'What do you have for us today?'

'I have prepared a monologue.'

'That's not what we want.'

'Tell us your secrets.'

'You must.'

'Give us the truth.'

'This is your last chance.'

'Tell us what you know.'

A stack of papers hurtles down from above you and lands at your feet. A script?

'This is your audition!'

'Just play the part!'

You begin.

About Ixtab Media

We are an independent publishing house based in the North East of England, but with rogue cells in several other cities around the world. It seemed like a global pandemic was the best time to start a publishing company. Our goals can be summed up as follows:

Create engaging, experimental work larger companies won't touch

Promote and encourage more marginalised groups of writers, i.e. *everyone* from a working-class background, regardless of skin colour, orientation, or (insert anything here)

Develop new IPs that explore community, camaraderie, and interpersonal relations in a way everyone can enjoy, and then perhaps realise our problems stem from fundamental world problems rather than some malevolent Other

Sell all these IPs to Netflix and use that money to generate even more content people of all backgrounds can enjoy

Support free speech and stimulate fresh ideas

Generate earnest debate

Support writers, artists, and editors with a viable, co-op style approach to our finances

Allow easy access to our literature for the less fortunate

Failing that, we'd like to create art we'd like to consume ourselves. At a time where it feels everything can be commodified, sterilised, and sold back to us by giant corporations, it's imperative we foster a place where risks can be taken, and truths can be told. Reading this far is help enough, but if you feel like buying large quantities of our books, we're fine with that too.

A sincere thank you from all of us for reading this far.

www.ingramcontent.com/pod-product-compliance
Lightning Source LLC
Chambersburg PA
CBHW032017050726
47590CB00006B/2211